He stood six feet tall...

with broad shoulders under an open white doctor's coat that showed tight jeans and cotton shirt underneath. Sandy brown hair in need of a trim was brushed straight back from his angular face.

Definitely attractive—in a rugged sort of way that human women like, thought Angelina the fairy godmother. Even the faint scar on his chin added to the mystery about him. Yes, definite possibilities...until she noticed the little boy staring up at him and heard the child call him "Daddy."

There was no way Dr. Ben Grant and Reggie Clark were a match made in heaven—or anywhere. Children weren't part of Reggie's life plan. Angelina was looking at her only failure, for sure. "I may be a fairy godmother," she muttered, "but I'm not in the miracle business!"

Dear Reader,

Their ideal bedtime story starts with a deep voice saying, "Hey, gorgeous," not "Once upon a time." To them, "baby" is an endearment, not a stage of life! Yep, Reggie Clark is about to get a wake-up call. She's about to become an "Accidental Mom"!

Mary Anne Wilson takes you on a hilarious ride into parenthood—as careerwoman Reggie Clark learns a thing or two from pediatrician Ben Grant and his young handful, a.k.a. "son"—all with a little help from her well-meaning guardian angel!
Mary Anne Wilson is the recipient of many awards for romantic suspense; here she clearly shows she's equally adept at humor!

Don't miss the companion novel to this—
Lisa Bingham's *The Daddy Hunt*—available right now!

Happy reading!

Debra Matteucci
Senior Editor and Editorial Coordinator
Harlequin Books
300 East 42nd Street
New York, NY 10017

Mary Anne Wilson

MISMATCHED MOMMY?

Harlequin Books

TORONTO • NEW YORK • LONDON
AMSTERDAM • PARIS • SYDNEY • HAMBURG
STOCKHOLM • ATHENS • TOKYO • MILAN
MADRID • WARSAW • BUDAPEST • AUCKLAND

For Herb Bignell—

One of the most
important men in my life.

Thanks for everything, Dad.
I love you.

ISBN 0-373-16652-4

MISMATCHED MOMMY?

Copyright © 1996 by Mary Anne Wilson.

Chapter One

One minute, Angelina was on Bourbon Street in New Orleans, admiring the very successful conclusion of her last assignment. The next thing she knew, she was being pulled back, flashing to headquarters and directly into the reflection room. She hated being zapped like that.

As she materialized in the huge, mirror-lined space, classical music replaced the noise and celebration of New Orleans. The scent of roses replaced the unique odors of Bourbon Street. She had barely settled on the thick white carpet, when she saw Miss Victoria standing in the middle of the space. She was very still, just staring at Angelina with a faint look of distaste on her face.

Any satisfaction Angelina had felt at finally getting the cowboy and the snake dancer together was short-lived. Miss Victoria was the head of everything. And everyone knew she never demanded meetings like this unless something was very wrong. If Angela had to guess, she knew what it was. She knew the liberties she'd taken with the ground rules in New Orleans. But no one, even Miss Victoria, could argue with the outcome.

"Really, Angelina, is that any way to dress?" the tiny woman finally said as she adjusted rimless glasses. "Denim jeans and a…a…" She waved one tiny hand at Angelina. "What is that thing you're wearing?"

"A tank top, ma'am," Angelina supplied quickly.

"A tank top," Miss Victoria echoed as if the words were foreign to her. Then her blue eyes flicked to Angelina's hair. The flame-colored mane was loose around her shoulders and falling partway down her back. "And your hair?"

Angelina kept from brushing at it. "I…I should have braided it, but—"

One sniff from Miss Victoria cut off any apology.

"That smell. What is it?"

Angelina inhaled and grimaced. "Oh, that's beer, ma'am. This friend of the subject was celebrating, and well, I had materialized and he bumped into me."

The frown on Miss Victoria's face deepened.

"I know, I wasn't supposed to be there right then, but I felt it was necessary for the successful completion of the assignment. And it was successful, ma'am, very successful."

"So, the ends justify the means?" the other woman muttered with a shake of her head. "We know it was agreed in the council that we would try to fit into the mortal world and stop all the fairy and sprite misconceptions. But one has to wonder if it is a good idea to fit in too well."

Angelina braced herself for a lecture on the old ways, on the sad passing of sparkle and magic, images that fitted in with fairy tales. To fend it off, she spoke quickly. "I know I owe you an apology about New Orleans, but I really felt that I had to use some latitude to be successful."

Miss Victoria held up one hand that glittered with diamonds, and stopped the explanation. "We are aware of the fact that things have to be done a bit differently now. We do not have a uniform rule anymore, and you are the new level. We understand that." She glanced down at her own clothes, a simple blue, ankle-length dress trimmed in white eyelet ruffles and worn with black slippers. "Ah, but the old ways..." Miss Victoria sighed heavily, then shook her head sharply. "But times have changed and we must change with them if we are to help those we are meant to serve."

"Yes, ma'am," Angelina murmured. The new-level workers never had that concept of serving, just doing. And she did this work because she'd never known anything else. Besides, she was good at it and she got such a rush out of doing it well, the way she just had done. "About New Orleans, ma'am," she said.

"We don't have time for that right now," Miss Victoria said as she moved one hand and a soft chime sounded. At the same time, the mirrored wall to Angelina's right shifted and changed until it looked like a giant screen of shimmering lights. Gradually images began to form.

"There is a situation that just came to our attention and we knew that you were the one to take care of it. Since you have just finished an assignment, we called you back so you can get started right away. Time is of the essence."

It wasn't about New Orleans, or about her clothes and hair, and Angelina almost sighed with relief, until she saw the image on the screen. She'd barely covered a gasp, when she recognized the store in downtown Santa Barbara where old and rare books were bought, sold and restored. And in the middle of the scene of leather and wood and a few people browsing quietly among the stacks was the only failure Angelina had ever had in this business.

"Regina Louise Clark," Miss Victoria said from somewhere off to the right.

But Angelina never took her eyes off the scene in front of her. Regina Clark was at a desk in a back room of the store, bent over her work, restoring what appeared to be a very slender book. With great expertise, she carefully applied leather to the spine. Reggie, who looked just the way Angelina remembered her being two years ago. Her long chestnut hair was caught in a simple twist at her nape. Her oval face, makeup free, was dominated by wide-set amber eyes, and her full lips were fixed in a straight line of serious contemplation.

"You remember her, of course," Miss Victoria said.

"Yes...yes, I remember," she murmured. Who ever forgot failure? Who ever forgot their only flaw?

"Reggie—that is what she calls herself, isn't it?"

Angelina took a deep breath as she watched Reggie meticulously adhering the leather to the book spine. "Yes, it is. Or she used to."

"Whatever she calls herself now," Miss Victoria said quietly, "she needs our help. Our immediate help."

Reggie looked as she always had, content surrounded by books...and peace and quiet. Doing what she loved. Alone. "I don't see what could be—"

"Shush," Miss Victoria said, cutting off Angelina's words. "Listen."

A phone rang and Reggie carefully set the book down in the work area, then reached for the phone to her right. "Jefferson and Davis Rare Book Restoration. How may I help you?"

Angelina couldn't hear the voice on the other end of the line, but she could see the way Reggie smiled suddenly. She saw the faint blush that touched her high cheekbones and the way she sat back with a sigh. "Oh, Dennis, hello."

Angelina knew that look well, but had never seen it on Reggie. Ever.

"Well, I'll be. I thought the council decided that Reggie was one of the rare humans who actually did better alone. But it seems she's found someone after all." She cast Miss Victoria a slanted look, feeling relief flooding over her. "Someone I introduced into her life?" she asked hopefully. "Maybe Martin, the Italian fellow from Los Angeles?"

"No, he's involved with some movie star now. Happily involved, we believe."

"Then who?"

"Dennis Benning," Miss Victoria said as Reggie laughed softly and spoke into the phone. "Tax attorney, thirty-four, very attractive—by human standards—and available. Actually, a lovely man in a lot of ways, very stable, settled, a peaceable sort for a human being."

"That sounds like a match made in—"

Miss Victoria cut her off with a sharp look, then said, "Right now Mr. Benning is asking her out for dinner tonight. He intends to tell her he wants her to meet his parents. Which means a marriage proposal, if she passes muster, is imminent."

Angelina felt the weight of her only failure begin to fall from her shoulders. Reggie was saying, "I'd love to, Dennis."

So, it was all going to work out after all. "Is he in our program?" she asked as Reggie hung up and sat back in the leather chair with a dreamy smile on her face.

"No. The man has never come to our attention until now. It seems he has his own plans for a career and marriage. And he's been doing just fine without our help." Miss Victoria sighed. "Very efficient, as far as humans go."

Angelina turned back to Miss Victoria. "If this is all settled, I don't understand why you called me in."

Miss Victoria looked as if she feared for Angelina's sanity. "My dear, we believe he is totally wrong for her."

Angelina could feel her jaw drop, but couldn't stop it. "But you said that—"

"He's going to ask her to marry him as soon as his parents give him their stamp of approval. She fits into his plans, and he fits into what she thinks she wants."

Angelina knew she was missing something in this conversation. "He is interested in women, isn't he?"

"Interested?" Miss Victoria asked vaguely, then her eyes widened behind her spectacles. "Oh, yes, of course."

"Then Mr. Benning seems to be offering Reggie what she wants. Order and peace in her life. A plan, not the chaos she had growing up. The poor girl was burned out on noise and confusion, on a life that was always topsy-turvy. Mr. Benning seems very defined and neat."

"If tonight goes well, he plans on asking her to marry him on Thanksgiving, five days away, and when he does, she *will* accept, and she *will* stay with him forever."

"But, ma'am, isn't that our goal?"

Wrong question. Angelina knew that as soon as the words were out and Miss Victoria shook her head with a soft "Tsk, tsk, tsk. We think, when this is finished, you should consider signing up for a refresher class in objectives. The only 'forever' in this business is happiness. And that does not come from being paired with the wrong person forever."

"Ma'am, I just meant that if Mr. Benning is so nice... I mean, there's nothing wrong with him—"

"Of course there's nothing wrong with him per se, but he's not right for her. And it's up to us to give her the opportunity to know what she *could* have. We need to at least offer her a very significant option, and even if she chooses not to take it, she can never say she never had the chance. Her life won't be filled with what-ifs or she won't have to live with that niggling feeling some humans endure that she missed something more, but doesn't know what it was."

"If Mr. Benning isn't the one, and none of the several *very* adequate men I put into her life was the one, then who is?"

Miss Victoria waved a hand at the shimmering wall. "Dr. Benjamin Grant."

Angelina knew that name—she'd heard it before—and as she turned to look at Reggie dissolving and being replaced by a new image, she knew where she'd heard the name. He was Hope's project.

The scene had changed to what appeared to be a make-believe forest, with trees painted on walls, clouds floating on ceilings, and tables and chairs that resembled something out of a cartoon classic. But in the middle was an unmistakable doctor's examination table. On closer observation, one could see carefully disguised cupboards along the walls, partially hidden by cutouts of trees and bushes, and a sink in the middle of a green counter framed by picket fencing.

A little boy with a Buster Brown cap of blond hair and a cherubic face with huge brown eyes sat on the table dressed in denim overalls and a striped red

T-shirt. He couldn't have been more than two years old, and he was solemnly regarding the man standing close to him. A band of information ran along the bottom of the screen.

"Dr. Benjamin Grant, thirty-five years of age, single, never married."

Dr. Benjamin Grant. A man about six feet tall, with broad shoulders under an open white doctor's coat that showed Levi's and a cotton chambray shirt underneath. Sandy brown hair that was in bad need of a trim was brushed straight back from an angular face. He rested one hand on the little boy's shoulder, and his other hand cupped the child's chin to tip his face up.

"Now, Mikey," he was saying with quiet earnestness. "It's okay. We'll get another batch of tongue depressors. But the next time, no fort building with them. Okay?"

"Me sorry," the child whispered.

The man was definitely attractive, in a rugged sort of way that human women liked, and Angelina knew that Reggie had never been into "pretty" men. A good doctor and very kind, obviously. He wasn't even angry the boy had ruined his supplies. He seemed a peaceable sort, quiet of manner and orderly.

When Mikey's bottom lip began to tremble, the doctor picked the boy up and hugged him to his chest.

"Hey, it's okay, it's okay," he soothed as he patted the child's back.

"Ah, he seems nice," Angelina said. "But Dr. Grant is Hope's assignment."

"He was. Until she failed miserably."

Angelina watched Ben Grant hold the boy back, then reach with his free hand for a sucker from a sunflower dish on the sink. As he offered it to the child, he smiled. A lovely smile. He'd be so easy for Angelina to place. Maybe Reggie would see the possibilities. That faint scar on his chin was attractive, added a bit of mystery. Yes, he had definite possibilities.

But that thought was dashed when the little boy smiled and grabbed the sucker. "Tank oos, Daddy."

Daddy? She looked at Miss Victoria. "What did he call that man?"

"'Daddy.'"

"But it says he's not married."

"One doesn't have to be married to be a parent, Angelina, and Dr. Grant has never been married. He's too involved with his work. Hope set him up a number of times, but he never even showed for the meets. He is crazy about kids, and he's known as one of the best pediatricians in the state."

"Pediatrician?" Angelina repeated in a weak voice. "Kids?"

"Yes, and he's always wanted a big family of his own, lots of kids. I guess that's why he adopted Michael Benjamin Grant four months ago. 'A single-parent adoption,' I think they call it. They make a wonderful pair. And Dr. Grant is seriously considering adopting more children."

This was going from bad to worse. "Ma'am, that's lovely. But that's exactly why he and Reggie are so . . . so different. Children aren't part of her plans."

"Excuse me?"

"She actually loves kids. She always has. But she just doesn't want any. She turned down a second date with two of the men I set her up with because they had little ones. The Italian gentleman with three kids was a very charming man, just like Ben Grant, but she told him that she had enough of caring for kids. As the eldest daughter in a family of nine, she was a built-in second mother. She's done it all and doesn't want to do it again. And it looks as if Dr. Grant is intent on having a lot of kids...one way or the other."

Before Miss Victoria could say anything else, Angelina jumped in boldly with both feet. "I think this is a lost cause, ma'am, and maybe this Dennis Benning would be a more suitable match for Reggie. I don't see how she and Dr. Grant could get together. I really don't."

Miss Victoria just looked at her and slowly shook her head. "Oh, Angelina, we *are* disappointed in you. After all the, er, ingenuity you showed in New Orleans, we expected so much more from you."

Angelina hated that look and tone. "Ma'am, there's only so much I can—"

"Oh, very well, we shall make this a bit easier for you." She waved her hand imperiously toward the screen, but nothing happened. "Now the rest is up to you."

"I don't see what—"

"You shall," Miss Victoria said, and nodded at the screen. "Just watch."

Angelina glanced back at the scene in the doctor's office, where Ben was trying to avoid having the sucker pushed into his mouth by the toddler. A nurse peered into the office. "Sorry to bother you, Doctor."

"What is it, Brenda?" Ben Grant asked before he reluctantly took a taste of the sucker.

"Your real-estate agent called. The house you were interested in on Echo Ridge unexpectedly came on the market and she needs you to meet her there as quickly as possible. The people who own it decided to move and are in a great hurry to sell."

Ben evaded another thrust of the sucker. "Is she serious?"

"That's what she said. But she needs you to meet her at the house at six."

"Tell her I'll be there," Ben said, then eyed the boy. "Well, Mikey, it looks as if we might have just hit the jackpot. You remember that big old house we found up in the hills?" He sat the child on the counter by the sink and started washing his sticky hands with paper towels. "The nice people who said they would never think of selling it for at least a year—Mr. and Mrs. Eaton—well, they suddenly want to go ahead."

The little boy solemnly watched Ben. "More candy?"

"No way. You've had enough." He grinned down at Mikey. "And we have to get going. Hey, with any luck, we'll be able to move in by Christmas." He picked his son up and headed for the door. "Let's get you home to Nancy so I can get there by six."

"Go see Nana?" Mikey asked.

"Right now," Ben said as they went out the door.

"Nancy?" Angelina asked.

"His housekeeper-baby-sitter. And she shan't be available to keep the boy."

The screen began to dissolve, until just the mirrors were in place, and Angelina turned. "How do you know that she won't be able to..." She bit her lip. "Oh, I see. That's the help you gave me?"

"Part of it. The other half is the house coming on the market. It's right next door to Regina's on Echo Ridge above Santa Barbara. It's a perfect house, two stories, old, rambling, perfect for Dr. Grant and the boy and the others he'll eventually bring there. Margaret and Horace Eaton have owned it all their married lives, for fifty-one years, and raised their five children there. Now they're going to Florida to be closer to their grandchildren and great-grandchildren."

"You sound as if you knew them."

"We did...fifty-one years ago." She smiled slightly. "Now, there was a pair of humans who seemed like oil and water. It was a difficult assignment, but it certainly paid off. And it appears that it has worked out well for everyone involved, especially Dr. Grant and Regina."

Angelina had seldom thought of Miss Victoria working in the field. It seemed odd someway to realize that fifty-one years ago, she'd been in much the same position Angelina was in now. "Yes, it appears for the best," she murmured.

"Okay, you have a start in this assignment." She lifted one fine eyebrow in Angelina's direction. "We shall leave the rest of it in your hands. Remember that most humans don't know what they want until they fall over it. Just give them a chance at happily ever after, my dear. Now, go and take care of things."

"Happily ever after," Angelina echoed, then turned and headed for the door.

"Oh, Angelina?"

She stopped and looked back over her shoulder. "Yes, ma'am?"

"The clothes...we think it is wise for you to re-think them. Santa Barbara is a bit chilly in November—at least it was the last time I was there."

"Yes, ma'am," Angelina said, and left the office. As she closed the door behind her and stood in the silent, mirrored corridor, she caught sight of her reflection and grimaced. "Reggie and Ben Grant," she muttered. "Oil and water? Try night and day." She exhaled and brushed at her hair. "I'm not in the miracle business."

"No, we are in the opportunity business, Angelina," Miss Victoria's disembodied voice echoed around her.

Angelina was startled by the sound and looked behind her, but the door was firmly closed. Quickly she turned and headed for her space. Ben and Reggie. Oil and water. Night and day. Her stomach sank as she realized she was walking right into failure number two of her career. Both of them at the hands of Regina Clark.

As she slipped into her space and started to change for the assignment, she shook her head. Ben and Reggie would get together when cows could fly. And even Miss Victoria couldn't make that happen.

At least, Angelina didn't think she could.

Chapter Two

"Mr. Perfect? You're thinking of marrying Mr. Perfect? Egad, Reg." Reggie's younger sister Melanie almost shrieked over the phone line. "Tell me you don't mean it."

Reggie grimaced at her sister's jab, but had to admit that the term "Mr. Perfect" fitted Dennis Benning, well, perfectly.

In fact, the first thing Reggie had noticed when Dennis had walked into the bookstore six months ago was how perfect he looked. Blond hair with a razor cut framed an even-featured face dominated by gray eyes and a wide mouth, with just the suggestion of a cleft in his clean-shaven chin. His clothes looked as if he'd just stepped off the pages of *GQ*— well cut, expensive and immaculate. Even his voice was smooth and perfect. Yes, Mr. Perfect, with a great career as a tax attorney, a great house and a great life in front of him. And she knew she wouldn't mind being part of it.

"Okay, Dennis is perfect," Reggie allowed as she stood and faced the wardrobe door mirrors in her bedroom. "But he hasn't asked me to marry him. Not yet." She smoothed the straight skirt of her black velvet cocktail dress with her free hand. "I just said I think that's what he's going to do tonight. We've got reservations at La Domain for seven-thirty."

"Oh, Reg, that's terrible."

"It's a great restaurant, the most expensive in—"

"Not that. The idea of you marrying him."

"Aren't you the one who said she thought Dennis was . . . what was it, cute?"

"He is. Sort of. But you know the saying, cute is as cute does," her sister muttered. "He is also conservative and uptight and he actually likes that house of his with its white walls, white carpet and black marble. And that's where you'd live, you know. In that mausoleum, not in the neat bungalow you own."

Reggie glanced around the room, at the high ceilings, the plaster walls and the hardwood floors. It had taken her two months to find the bleached-wood poster bed, and she wasn't at all sure she wanted to just walk away from it. "It's hardly gone that far— yet. And Dennis is very...orderly and he's got his life under control. Unlike others, I might add, he isn't going off in a million pieces all the time."

"He's got a master plan for his life, for pete's sake. You told me that."

"Yes, he does." Reggie twisted to make sure the dress looked okay on her. After spending over a hundred dollars on it, she wanted to look as good as possible tonight. "And I like that."

"Can you live with the fact that you're part of a plan, that you fit a niche? Are you prepared to have two point five children to fall within the normal range of that plan?"

Reggie did laugh at that. "Dennis doesn't really want children. You know, some people do believe that two people can be happy without kids, and that they don't have to try for nine."

"Mom and Dad didn't try for nine—they just happened to have nine."

"It takes more than happenstance to have nine children," Reggie said as she smoothed her hair, which was caught in a low twist. The only good jewelry she owned was on her neck—a simple gold locket that Dennis had given her for her birthday two months ago. "And after living around ten other people for most of my life, I just want some peace and quiet."

"You know, Reg, I never understood you. You grew up in a big family with something happening all the time, and the first man you even consider marrying almost passed out the only time he met all of us. I mean, he actually grimaced when Teddy was going to toss him the football."

"He was dressed to go out, not to play touch football." Reggie glanced around the shadowy bedroom, the quiet, orderly room, then back to her reflection in the doors. The slender woman wearing an expensive dress, her chestnut hair in an elegant twist, her makeup understated, was a far cry from the Reggie she'd been most of her life. The child who had always felt she had no place to call her own finally had her own space. And maybe that place wasn't this house, but the life she could share with Dennis.

"He probably never ever played football."

"He's an only child and didn't have a built-in team living in his house. He's just not used to that sort of . . . of commotion."

"It's called 'family,' Reggie."

Reggie had a flashing cascade of memories of "family." Of being the second child of nine and the first girl, the one to take on the younger kids, the one to be surrogate mom when her mother was busy having another child. The child who had hidden in closets with a flashlight just to read the books she loved in peace. Until someone found her.

"I always felt I was different from the rest of you," she murmured—an admission that was vaguely startling to her.

But anything profound about it was lost on Mel, who laughed over the phone line. "Is that why you used to tell people you were adopted?"

"I just said it was a possibility. But no one ever believed me," Reggie replied, a smile tugging at her own lips now. "Not when Mom and Dad had a child every two years."

"So, are you going to marry Dennis or not?" Mel asked bluntly.

Reggie stared hard at herself in the mirror. "I don't know," she said. "I'll have to wait until he asks, then see what happens."

"Do you love him?"

The question took Reggie off guard and it startled ·
her that an answer wasn't forthcoming. Love? Who
wouldn't love Dennis Benning? She'd liked him from
the first. She liked the purpose she sensed in him, the
calm way he handled things, the order and sanity in his
life. She liked quiet dinners, fine wine and a shared
interest in books and music.

"Come on, Reg, you know—rockets going off, the
earth moving? Love."

She wasn't sure how to answer her sister, but was
spared the need to respond when she heard a crashing
sound echo into the bedroom from the back of the
house. "What in the—" she muttered.

"What's wrong?" Mel asked.

"The cats from next door got into my garden room
last week, and it sounds as if they're back out there
again."

"But you said the Eatons were in Florida, and don't
they usually board the cats when they go there? They
couldn't just leave them like that, Reg."

"Maybe it's a stray, but I've got to go see what's
going on. Love to everyone," she said, and hung up.

Before she could turn, there was another crashing
sound. Forgoing her shoes, she ran in her stocking
feet into the small hallway, then into the dark kitchen
and to the French doors that led out into the garden
room.

As she reached for the handle, she was startled by
another crashing sound, followed by a piercing
scream. This wasn't cats, she realized as she pulled the
door open and stepped down into the room that ran

the length of the back of her house. "Okay, Elvis and Elton, you cats have had it. I can't believe—"

But her words were cut short when she switched on the overhead lights and turned to the screened-in room. It was in shambles, with the green wrought-iron table that had held six clay pots of geraniums lying on its side. The pots and plants had been reduced to a pile of broken clay, potting soil and crushed blossoms. And in the middle of the havoc she saw the source of the destruction and the screaming cries.

It wasn't one of the huge gray cats the Eatons owned, but a little boy who was probably less than two years old, wearing denim overalls that were covered in dirt. His little face was bright red, scrunched hard producing screams, and his cap of fine blond hair was caked with soil.

Reggie stared at him. A child? Here? One of the reasons she had bought this house was the neighborhood—big houses on big acre lots and mostly older residents who'd been here forever. She was at the end of a dead-end street, and the block had no kids living on it.

Her only close neighbors were the Eatons, and they had grandchildren, even great-grandchildren. She hadn't known they were back, but they'd obviously returned with this child in tow. As the toddler took a choking breath, Reggie went into an automatic mode, intent on getting this over with quickly so she would be ready when Dennis came for her.

She crouched, then spoke in an even voice. "Hey, fella, it's okay. It's fine, really. Where are your grandma and grandpa?"

At the sound of her voice, the child turned huge brown eyes in Reggie's direction. Silent tears rolled down his flushed face and his bottom lip quivered. "Hey, it's okay, it's okay. Just don't cry again," she said as she held out her hands for him to come to her. She flashed a look through the screened-in area to her yard and the high hedges that defined the property lines between her place and the Eatons'. There were lights blazing in the old house, but there wasn't a soul outside.

"Daddy. Want Daddy," the child whispered on a breathless sob.

As Reggie looked back at him, the boy scrambled to his feet. Before Reggie knew what he was going to do, the little boy rushed at her, throwing himself at her chest. Her velvet dress was crushed in the grip of tiny hands covered with dirt, and the impact of his sturdy body sent Reggie reeling backward onto the hard, cold, tiled floor.

In less than a heartbeat she was on the ground, with the child prone on top of her and his face buried in her shoulder.

"Daddy. Want my daddy," he sobbed into the black velvet as his little body shook.

"Yeah, so do I," Reggie breathed as she tried to stand. But the child wouldn't let go. The best she could manage was to get to a sitting position, with her legs out in front of her and the boy in her lap. But his hold on her didn't lessen and neither did his crying.

"Daddy. Want my Daddy," he wailed.

She patted his back and automatically lowered her voice, telling him everything would be all right and trying to figure out how to get him off her so she could go get the Eatons.

"Okay, I'm just going to stand up," she murmured to the child, hoping she could get up without more screaming starting. "Now, be a good boy," she said, talking softly and constantly as she maneuvered. "Just stay calm, and this will all be over soon. I'll find your mom and dad or your grandma and grandpa and figure this out." She moved slowly, felt the wall at her back, but never made it to her feet.

Somewhere outside she heard someone shouting, "Mikey, where are you? Mikey?" A man's voice came from the outside, and the moment he shouted the name, the little boy moved quickly. He sat back, turned around, then scrambled off Reggie and ran for the back door. His little hands reached for the knob, but even stretching, he was a full three inches too short.

"Mikey!"

The little boy started to cry again, and Reggie called out over the noise to the man outside. "In here. He's in here."

Before she could get up, the door flew open, almost swiping the child backward. From her vantage point on the cold tile, Reggie saw a man all but lunge into the garden room. She had a blurred impression of denim and wide shoulders, brown hair, then the child was in his arms and being hugged tightly.

"Oh, Mikey, you scared me to death," the man declared.

The child squirmed back, then he pressed his tiny, dirty hands to the man's cheeks and sobbed, "Want to go home, Daddy. Peeze."

"You bet," the man said.

The man had his back partially to Reggie, and she discreetly cleared her throat to get his attention. Someone was going to have to pay for this mess. But when he turned and looked past the little boy at her, the mess was the last thing on her mind. If the man had been a blur before, he was exactly the opposite now.

His image seemed painfully clear. Dark-blue eyes under a slash of dark brows were set in a strong sharply angular face with a faint scar that hooked over his chin just below a mouth with a very sensuous bottom lip. Sandy brown hair was long enough to brush the collar of a chambray shirt being soiled by the boy's clothes, and the jeans worn with dark boots fitted snugly over strong thighs.

He was not handsome, not even close, but something about him disturbed her. And she didn't understand it, not any more than she understood the heat that she knew was touching her cheeks under his scrutiny. Anger came, self-defensive anger, and she muttered with a frown, "Is he yours?"

"He sure is," the man said.

His voice was deep and rough, and played havoc with her already frayed nerves.

"Did he do this?"

"All of it," she said tightly.

"He knocked you down?"

"He did it," she said. "Single-handedly."

"Wow," he breathed.

To Reggie this sounded suspiciously like admiration of the destruction his son had inflicted on her garden room.

"He couldn't have been gone more than five minutes."

"Five minutes too long," she said, nurturing the anger to keep some semblance of sanity in the situation.

"Mikey never ceases to amaze me."

"I bet," she mumbled, then knew she wanted up. She didn't wish to be looking up at this man any longer. She felt at a distinct disadvantage from this angle.

The moment she moved to get to her feet, the man shifted the boy to one hip and held out his free hand to her.

"Here, let me help."

She ignored his offer, not at all certain that she wanted to touch him, and not just because his hand was soiled from the child he was holding. "I didn't know that the Eatons were back." She flashed a narrowed look at man and child as she got to her feet and brushed her hands together. "Or that they brought company."

"They aren't here. They're in Florida," he said.

"Whatever." She glanced around at the mess, a very safe alternative to keeping contact with the man's blue eyes. "Your son did a lot of damage."

"How did he get in here anyway?"

"Just like the cats."

"Excuse me?"

"The Eatons' cats can push at the door until the lock clicks back. Your son must have done the same thing. Then the door shut on him."

He jiggled the boy on his hip. "This is your house?"

"Yes."

"A great old bungalow. This style always looked like a crouched lion to me, with the pillars on the front porch and the dormer just above the front part of the house."

She didn't want to discuss anything with this man except the damage that was lying at their feet. She swiped at her dress futilely and knew more was damaged than just pots and plants. "Oh, great," she muttered at the mud matting the velvet. "It's ruined."

"It sure is," he agreed readily.

She gazed up at him. "It cost a great deal."

"It looks very, er..."

His eyes flicked over her from head to foot, the action making her breathing catch uncomfortably in her chest. And by the time his eyes met hers again, she could feel the heat gathering in her cheeks once more, but not from anger this time.

"Very expensive," he finally finished, and held out his hand again. "I think we should introduce ourselves. I'm Ben, and this is Mikey."

Ben, a name that fitted him in some way. But she wasn't going to analyze it. Damn it, the man was the most uncomfortable person she'd been around in a very long time, no matter what his name was. She literally steeled herself as she reached out to take his hand. *Do it. Get it over with,* she told herself. But the moment they touched, that second when his fingers closed around her hand, her pep talk went out the window.

She stood very still, trying to absorb the way this man seemed to demand her total attention. And when a chiming sound came from nowhere, it took her a full heartbeat to realize the music hadn't been produced by his touch. Stupid, silly thought, she told herself. The doorbell. Her doorbell was ringing.

She drew back quickly from Ben. "The bell. The door chimes."

"Yes," he said with the hint of a smile in his blue eyes. "Your doorbell."

"Yes, the door," she said quickly as she moved back a bit. Dennis was here. "The door." Dennis. How could she have totally forgotten he was coming? "I need to answer it," she said when the chimes sounded again.

"Of course," Ben said. "And about all of this..."

He motioned with the hand that had touched her to the mess on the floor.

"I'll pay for everything."

His eyes flicked over her dress again and she could feel her stomach tighten.

"And the dress...have it cleaned. Just let me know what the costs are for everything."

The boy had settled against the man's shoulder, and his thumb had found its way into his mouth. Brown eyes regarded Reggie solemnly as the two adults were talking.

Ben held the boy back just a little to look into his face. "Mikey, tell the nice lady you're sorry."

The toddler ducked his head a bit, but muttered, "Sorry, wady," then pressed his face back into his father's shoulder.

"He was gone before I knew it, and he's very active." He shook his head. "I really am sorry."

Reggie sensed movement outside, then the door opened and Dennis was suddenly there, coming into the garden room. For a split second he was side by side with Ben and Mikey. A man in a perfectly cut camel's hair overcoat worn over a conservative dark suit with a cream-colored shirt and subdued red tie. Mr. Perfect, whose smile faltered when he looked at Reggie, then turned to the man and child next to him.

Ben, a man in soiled clothes, with mussed hair and a child with a runny nose hugging him hard, casually glanced from Dennis to Reggie, then back to Dennis again. But he didn't say a thing as he kept patting Mikey's back.

"Regina?" Dennis said finally. "I rang the bell, then came around here when you didn't answer. My God, what's going on here?"

Ben held tightly to Mikey, his relief that the boy was safe tempered by finding this woman with him. He'd heard the crying, and he hadn't thought twice about coming in to get his son, then he'd seen her. On the floor, mud and dirt on her dress, obviously from Mikey, and chestnut curls partially loosed from a diamond clip. Her face, delicately pretty, with amber eyes framed by lush lashes and a suggestion of freckles across the bridge of a short, straight nose, had seemed incredibly beautiful right then.

Long, slender legs were provocatively exposed where the skirt of the velvet dress was hiked up; her feet were bare except for fine hosiery, and her hands braced her in a sitting position. Almost without thinking, he'd noticed she wasn't wearing a ring, any at all. Then, as he'd met her gaze, he'd seen a distinctly stunned look in her amber eyes shift to annoyance and anger.

It had been a long time since Ben had looked at a woman and wanted to see her laugh. A long time since he'd wanted to free a woman's hair to see it lie against her skin, and a long time since he realized how very lonely his bed had been.

Words were said, but they seemed unimportant, then he had his hand out to her, wanting to touch her, yet having no reason to other than to help her to her feet. But she'd ignored his offer of help, and as she'd struggled to get up, he took a step back and drew his hand away. Then tried again. Holding out his hand he'd touched her.

There was a fleeting sense of delicate warmth, slender fingers, then chimes had sounded and he'd felt her stiffen. The contact was broken, and Ben wondered why he could still feel her hand in his even when he started to pat Mikey's back again. The touching hadn't been such a good idea. Not when that was all there was, and not when he wanted so much more.

He was talking to her, saying things that he hoped made sense, knowing he had to leave. It was an effort to sound casual as he apologized for the damage. And an effort not to smile and use a very well-used line from his deep, distant past. "So, what are you doing for the rest of your life?"

Then his chance was gone as a man came to the door. And as Ben turned to the intruder, he regretted not jumping in with both feet, the way Mikey usually did, and not worrying about decorum. Now it was too late.

The man, perfectly attired in very expensive clothes, stood there with a proprietorial air. A look of surprise on his picture-perfect face that shifted to disgust when he eyed Mikey and the mess made Ben want to do a very undoctorlike rearrangement of his features.

"Who are these people, Regina?" the man asked in a tone laced with distaste. "And what's going on?"

"Dennis, I'm sorry. There's been a slight accident, and—"

Dennis shifted his gaze to the woman and spoke tightly. "You look as if you've been in a mud fight."

Ben watched the exchange, the way the woman brushed ineffectively at the soiled dress and nervously tried to tuck her hair behind her ears.

"Dennis, I can explain later, but I need to change."

"We've got reservations for seven-thirty, and—"

"No problem. I'll be right back."

"Regina." Ben said the name that the man had called her, and watched as her amber eyes turned on him, wide and expectant. "I'll be in touch," he said. "Let me know what the damages are," he added, then tightened his hold on Mikey again and moved to the door. As he brushed past the man, he didn't miss the way the guy moved back to avoid contact.

Highly polished oxfords stepped in a pile of potting soil, and Ben couldn't resist saying to the man just before he went out the door, "I'll pay to have your shoes polished, if you want."

He had a brief moment of satisfaction when the guy looked down with muted horror, then he was outside with Mikey, crossing the grass to the hedges. Then he stepped onto the next property and headed toward the huge old house that was going to be their home.

And by the time he met the real-estate agent at the front door, he realized something had happened that he hadn't been expecting. A neighbor. A woman whose presence had hit him like a bolt of lightning out of the blue. Regina. "Regina," he said softly.

Chapter Three

"Dr. Grant, oh, thank goodness you found the boy."

Ben looked up and saw Angie, the real-estate agent who had come in place of the woman he'd been working with, at the top of the steps on the wraparound porch. Tall, thin, with flame-red hair and wearing a red suit that was brilliant against the white of the old house, she turned to him and smiled.

She came down the steps to meet him on the short sidewalk that connected the porch area to the circular driveway, where he'd parked his Jeep. "I was certain he was fine. This old neighborhood is a very safe place. But where did you find him?"

"He was at the bungalow next door."

"Ah, a lovely house." She smiled widely. "I just know you're going to love this place."

Ben put Mikey down, and as the boy headed for the steps, he looked up at the wood-sided house and the grounds, then to the hedge that separated his place from the single-story bungalow beyond. "It seems pretty nice," he murmured.

"Dr. Grant, there was a call on the cell phone in your car. I heard it when I was out searching for the child and answered it. I hope you don't mind." She didn't pause to find out if he did or not. "Someone named Brenda said that a Mrs. Armstrong wants a meeting this evening."

Ruth Armstrong was the main contributor to the pediatric clinic Ben had been trying to get off the ground for the past year, the wife of a very important man with lots of money. And when the wife called, you didn't ask questions. "Thanks, I'll phone her and—"

Angie flipped open a notebook Ben hadn't been aware she was holding. "I wrote it all down for you. She wants you to meet her at La Domain, seven-thirty. She's made all the arrangements, and she said to come ready to talk." She glanced at Ben. "Something about a new funding program she wants to go over with you."

Mikey was running back and forth on the porch, making noises like an airplane, and Angie turned to look at him ripping around behind her, as she closed the notebook with a snap. "Little Mikey seems to feel right at home here."

"Yes, he does," Ben said, and knew that this place could really be home for the two of them.

"If you buy it, I'd put up a six-foot-high fence," Angie said as she turned back to Ben and flashed a big smile. "I forgot how . . . inventive a two-year-old can be."

Ben looked back at the house next door when he heard the rumble of a car starting. Then a black car backed onto the street, a powerful-sounding BMW sedan. As it turned to head back down the street, Ben caught a glimpse of the passenger. For a split second he saw her clearly in the dimness, her hair back in an elegant twist. She was wearing something pale now, sitting by side with the guy. Then she was gone.

"Nice neighbors," Angie murmured. "The Eatons said that they loved the woman who lived next door, a real sweetheart. I'm sure you'll love this neighborhood."

Ben felt Mikey grab his leg, and he reached down to lift the boy as the taillights of the BMW disappeared from sight. "It seems nice," he said, knowing it would be all too easy to fall in love with this place and the surroundings. But maybe not too smart.

"How about it, Dr. Grant? Do you think you're interested? Because if you aren't, we need to get moving on getting other clients out here to see it."

"I'm interested," Ben said as he turned and swung Mikey up into his arms. "Offer the Eatons ten thousand less than the asking price."

"And if they won't budge?"

Ben hesitated. Then, somewhere between Mikey patting him softly as the little boy snuggled into his shoulder and his remembering the amber eyes, he knew what he was going to do. "I'll pay their price."

"Excellent," Angie said, then added, "now we need to get back so you can find someone to watch the child while you make your appointment."

Ben glanced at the flame-haired woman. "Excuse me?"

"It sounded like an important meeting, and I just assumed that since you're single and the child is...uh—"

"Inventive?"

"Exactly," she said with that huge smile again. "I assumed that you'd need to find a baby-sitter. I remember you saying your nanny was gone for the day."

"The nanny will be back anytime now, and if I hurry, I can make the meeting."

Angie clapped her hands once, then said, *"Très bien."* For a moment she seemed a bit confused, then she shrugged. "How strange. I just got back from New Orleans and I guess that city just gets into one's blood."

"Sure," Ben said as he started with Mikey toward the car. "I guess so."

Angelina followed the man and the boy and couldn't help smiling. If she was right, the meeting had gone well, despite the fact the child had created a havoc she hadn't foreseen. Reggie had definitely noticed Ben, and he had definitely noticed her. Angelina could sense the electricity in the air. A good start. Very good.

As she got in the doctor's Jeep, she watched him fasten the boy in his car seat, then Ben slid in behind the wheel and started the car. She'd have to learn to drive one of these times, she thought as she sank back in the seat.

For an assignment she'd thought would be hard to get off the ground, it was going rather well. Ben glanced at her, and she smiled as he said, "Tell me more about the neighbors."

"I'm not at all familiar with the neighbors, since this isn't my usual location. I'm only doing this because Bernice got such a cold all of a sudden."

"Oh," Ben said as he backed out of the drive and headed down the street. "I thought you might know a bit, since you mentioned the woman next door."

She peered at him. "Well, come to think of it, I did hear that she bought the house a year or so ago."

"You wouldn't know if she's married or anything, would you?"

"Oh, I see."

He gave her a quick look. "What?"

"Children. You wonder if she has kids."

"Yeah, sure, kids."

"No, I don't believe so. In fact, I think I was told that there aren't many kids in the neighborhood. And, if I'm not mistaken, the woman next door is single. She lives there alone."

"Single?" Ben asked.

"That's what I've heard," Angelina said.

As Ben brushed his jaw with the tips of his fingers and murmured "I see," Angelina thought that there was a distinct possibility that cows might fly sooner or later.

"THE LITTLE HOOLIGAN," Dennis muttered as they stepped through the massive wooden front doors of La

Domain, a luxurious restaurant housed in a sprawling multistoried Spanish mansion set on a bluff over the ocean. They were in the reception area, which was topped by a thirty-foot domed ceiling and highlighted by polished oak flooring and deep burgundy walls. "I thought you said that there weren't any kids around your neighborhood."

"There haven't been," Reggie murmured. The angelic-looking child, with his blond cap of hair and huge brown eyes, didn't seem anything like a hooligan. But the memory of her topsy-turvy garden room soon banished that thought. "If I'd known the Eatons were going to have some of their family staying there with children, I would have locked everything up tight."

"Put padlocks on everything," Dennis said as he helped Reggie slip off her lightweight navy wool coat in the foyer. "The father seems unable to control the kid at all."

Reggie was surprised that the image of the father came to her with a clarity that was almost unreal. Blue eyes. The way his lips teased with the hint of a smile that hadn't materialized. The way he held the child close and patted his back.

She turned away from Dennis under the pretext of looking around the restaurant, at its overt elegance, with dark antiques making the place resemble a private mansion. But even feigned interest in the massive reception desk to one side of a broad archway to the main restaurant couldn't quite block the images of the father and child from her mind.

"Can't we change the subject?" she asked.

Dennis came up behind her and touched her shoulders, getting so close to her ear she felt his breath fan her skin as he spoke.

"Yes, we absolutely can. We have much nicer things to talk about than those two." He tightened his hold on her shoulders just a bit. "I've been looking forward to this all day."

Reggie touched his hand on her left shoulder, needing that connection to get some focus on reality. "Me, too," she breathed.

The strains of an old standard played by a string ensemble with saxophone filtered into the foyer, and there were the muffled sounds of diners and waiters in the dining room beyond the entryway.

"Did I tell you how fantastic you look?" Dennis murmured.

Reggie had changed into an ice-blue silk dress with a straight skirt that brushed her knees. It wasn't as elegant as the ruined black velvet, with a high neckline in the front, a low V at the back and mere caps for sleeves. But it was the next best dress in her wardrobe.

She shifted away from his touch and glanced back at Dennis. But as she met his gaze, she blinked when it was overlaid by another look—blue eyes studying her soiled velvet dress, flicking over her in a way that touched off just the beginning of that uneasiness with their owner. Suddenly she felt grateful that Dennis was so...so peaceable, so solid and predictable; felt thankful that looking into his eyes didn't make her stomach churn or her breathing tighten.

Impulsively she kissed Dennis on his cheek. "Thank you," she whispered.

She turned and glanced into the main room, a space with intimate table arrangements that used the ocean view to best advantage and lush greenery to define each separate area. Into the reception area stepped a tall woman dressed in a long black gown, who smiled at them as she approached. The only color on her person came from her hair—brilliant coppery curls that were swept up on the sides by diamond clips. "Welcome to La Domain. May I help you?"

"Benning. Reservations for two at seven-thirty," Dennis said.

"Mr. Benning. Yes indeed." She motioned to the room behind her. "Please, follow me," she invited. She took them to a table by the windows, framed by potted palms, and motioned them to the high-backed red leather chairs. "Your server will be with you in a moment."

Dennis helped Reggie into her chair, then went around to take the seat facing her. As he settled, she saw the source of the music; a room off the main area that looked as if it had once been a solarium held the small group of musicians. A scattering of couples danced slowly to the mellow sounds of the sax and strings, and overhead, a glass-domed ceiling let in the view of the night sky.

Reggie turned to Dennis to mention it to him, but the hostess came back right then. "I do apologize, but your server is busy for a moment. Can I get you something to drink?''

"I left orders for a bottle of champagne," Dennis said.

"Oh, yes, of course," the woman said. "The wine steward will bring it right away." Then she was gone.

As soon as they were alone, Dennis reached across the table to cover Reggie's hand with his. He smiled, and she remembered her first reaction to that look when he'd brought in a rare edition of English essays to be rebound. Something settled in her and she smiled back at him.

"This is a lovely place," she murmured.

"As soon as they bring the champagne, I want to talk to you about something," he said, then drew back as the hostess came across to their table.

"Sir, I'm so sorry to interrupt you," she said in a discreet whisper.

"What is it?" Dennis asked tightly.

"There is a phone call for you, sir," she said in a low voice, and held out a cordless phone to him, the mouthpiece covered with her other hand.

"Who is it?" Dennis asked, without taking it.

"The gentleman didn't say, sir. Just that it was very important and that he had to talk directly to you."

Dennis took the phone and blocked the mouthpiece with the palm of his hand. "Thanks," he said, then as the hostess hurried off, he looked at Reggie. "I don't know what this is about. No one but Mother and Father know that I'm here, and they know better than to call unless it's a real emergency."

"Then it has to be very important," Reggie said.

"It had better be a flaming emergency," he muttered, then put the phone to his ear. "Benning here," he said into the mouthpiece.

Reggie watched Dennis, not at all certain that she'd ever seen him this annoyed. Anger and Dennis just didn't seem to belong in the same sentence. Yet, as he listened to the person on the other end of the line, a frown tugged his eyebrows together.

"What are you talking about?" he demanded in a low, clipped voice. "No, I don't think so."

Reggie looked out the multipaned windows at the dark ocean blending with the night sky. Rain was just beginning to streak the glass, and a partial moon was slipping behind racing clouds.

"Okay, okay, just hold on," Dennis finally said. "Fifteen minutes tops."

As Reggie looked back at him, he was laying the phone on the table with a thud. He fingered the phone as he said, "Regina, there's an emergency at the firm. I need to go down to the main office right away."

"An emergency?" Dennis was a tax attorney, and that hardly seemed to be a profession where there could be an immediate dilemma, especially in November. "What happened?"

"One of the firm's biggest clients has a problem that he insists has to be handled right now. And I'm the only one who's worked on his files recently. I need to get there as soon as possible."

When Reggie would have stood to leave, Dennis stopped her by covering her hand with his. "No, we aren't going. *I'm* going. It will take me only half an hour, forty-five minutes tops. I just have to get the files out for him to look at and show him a revision we made. Will you stay here and wait for me? I don't want this to ruin the evening, although, God knows, it's been rocky from the first."

Reggie curled her fingers around Dennis's. "We can do this another time. You've got business, and—"

"No." He tightened his hold on her. "I don't want to do this another time. Please, just stay for a while. I won't be long. I'll order something for you, and there's champagne coming." He smiled at her. "Please, just stay, then we can talk."

"Sure," she murmured. "I can wait."

"Good. Great." He stood, then came around the table to touch her chin with the tips of his fingers. "I'm very sorry about all this."

"I understand. Don't worry about it. Go ahead and fix the emergency. I'll be here when you get back."

He smiled down at her, then stooped and brushed a cool kiss across her forehead. "You're wonderful," he whispered, then turned and hurried across the room.

The hostess seemed to come from nowhere. She leaned down over Reggie much the way Dennis had just done. "I'm so sorry for this interruption. I know how special this evening is supposed to be. Why don't you let me get you some appetizers while you wait for your gentleman friend to come back?"

Reggie looked up at the woman, and for a moment could have sworn that they'd met before. But she'd never been here before. She shook her head, not understanding that feeling any more than she understood how the woman could know Dennis was coming back. "Mr. Benning told you—"

"It's up to you what you'd like. We have a full menu of appetizers, or we could bring you a sampler tray."

"Yes, that sounds fine, the sampler tray."

"Very good. The champagne will be here in a minute, and if you need anything else, don't hesitate to ask." Then she was gone with a smile and slight wave of her hand.

Reggie turned toward the windows and stared out at the misting rain and the night shrouding the ocean. She'd wait right here for Dennis to come back. Nothing about tonight was going the way she'd hoped it would. But Dennis was returning, and she was going to wait right there until he did.

BEN DROVE into the parking lot of La Domain five minutes late for his appointment with Ruth Armstrong. He pulled the Jeep up in front of the valet parking station, jumped out, tossed the keys to the attendant, called out his last name and broke into a run, heading through the misty rain for the massive doors.

He slowed only when he stepped into the elegant surroundings. He took a deep breath as he tugged at the cuffs of the brown tweed jacket he was wearing over a band-collared black shirt and pressed Levi's. He'd found toys stuffed in the pockets of his only real suit and one button missing. So this was the closest he could come to being dressed up. But one look at this place, and he knew he was very underdressed.

"Good evening, sir," someone said.

As Ben turned toward the reception desk, he saw a flame-haired woman coming toward him with a smile.

"Welcome to La Domain."

"I'm meeting Mrs. Ruth Armstrong," Ben said as he glanced at a huge grandfather clock by the doors. "And I'm five minutes late."

"Oh, yes. You must be Dr. Grant. Please, come with me," the woman said as she turned and led the way to a side room.

Ben followed her into a very intimate bar area, with old-fashioned booths separated by half walls topped by dark-green velvet curtains. She motioned him to a booth by the doors, and as he sat down, she said, "Mrs. Armstrong phoned to say she'd be here momentarily. Until then..." She lifted one hand and called, "Charles, please get Dr. Grant whatever he wishes from the bar."

As the woman left with an "Enjoy," the bartender, in a white shirt and a perfectly tied bow tie, took her place.

"What would you like, Dr. Grant?"

"Scotch, straight," he said, then sat back as the bartender headed over to the bar.

Ben looked around at the room, barely seeing the old-pub atmosphere, then exhaled. He thought he'd be late; now she was letting him cool his heels. He exhaled to ease his tension. He hated these dinners with Ruth Armstrong. They were always at her whim, at her command, anytime, day or night. But if the clinic was going to be more than a dream, he knew he'd be wherever he had to be, whenever he had to be there.

Right now, if he had his druthers, he'd be at home with Mikey. As that thought formed, "home" was the house in the hills with its large rooms, huge yard and a neighbor with amber eyes.

He shook his head. She was single; he knew that. Her first name was Regina; he knew that. And he knew that for the first time in a very long time, he had looked at a woman with more than passing interest. That brought a rueful smile. Passing interest? Hell, she brought fantasies with her that were anything but passing.

Then he remembered Dennis, whoever he was, and his smile faltered. Nothing in life was simple. He'd learned that early on. And he had a hunch that anything to do with Regina with those amber eyes wouldn't be easy at all. God knows his reaction to her was so confused that he was hard put to sort it out beyond his physical response, which was crystal clear.

He took the scotch when the bartender put it in front of him, and sipped it. It wasn't like Ruth Armstrong to be late for one of her dinners. As he finished the drink, he looked at his watch. Fifteen minutes late now. Not like her at all. He motioned away a refill by the bartender, who seemed to hover, then took his cell phone out of his jacket pocket to call Ruth to make sure nothing was wrong. But when he flipped the phone open, he heard the faint beep and saw the low-battery light flashing.

"Dr. Grant," the hostess said as she approached his table. "Mrs. Armstrong just phoned and said to go ahead and be seated for dinner. She's been delayed, but she'll be here as soon as possible."

"Thanks," Ben said as he slipped the phone back in his jacket pocket.

"If you'll come with me, I'll show you to your table," the hostess said.

Ben took out his wallet and laid some bills on the table as he stood, then asked, "Do you have a phone I could use for a local call?"

"Of course, sir. I can bring one to your table."

"I'd appreciate it," he said, then asked, "where's the men's room?"

"Down the side hallway on the left."

"I'll be back in a minute," he said, then stepped past her to head for the hallway.

"Let me know when you wish to be seated," the hostess called after him.

Ben waved a hand in her general direction, then walked out of the bar and saw the hallway to the right. He spotted a discreet sign for the men's room, and wished he were leaving now. But he knew he wouldn't go, not with Ruth Armstrong's goodwill at stake. He'd do whatever it took to get her contribution to the clinic, and if that meant waiting here for a while, so be it.

As he stepped into the men's room, he had a strange thought that came from nowhere. He would have waited anywhere for his new neighbor. Anywhere and for any amount of time. He had a bizarre flash in that moment of him waiting in the house, quietly watching, then having her come to him. A sense of something he couldn't begin to define accompanied the images, yet when he shook his head sharply, the image exploded in his mind.

It wasn't waiting—it was finding. It was realizing that she was there, that she was coming to him, and that in that moment, he wanted nothing more than to be right there with her. He crossed to the sinks, turned on the water and splashed coolness on his face. God, just a thought of her and he could feel his body betraying him on a very basic level.

Damn it, he told himself as he stared at his face in the mirror. "You've been out of the loop for way too long," he muttered, then grabbed one of the folded towels on the sink and scrubbed the white cotton over his face. "Business, business, business," he said, and pushed those errant thoughts out of his mind.

Chapter Four

Reggie sipped champagne and nibbled at a stuffed mushroom cap as she watched the couples in the dance area under the rain-streaked glass dome. Slow music, soft lights and a rainy night. So romantic, she mused. Then she glanced out the windows to her right and saw her own reflection, distorted by the rain. A woman with champagne and music... and alone.

Then she saw someone else in the reflection, someone across the way, in the entry area, a distorted image in the thick glass of the windows. Unrecognizable. But for a crazy moment, she thought it was the man from earlier, Mikey's father. Something about the way he walked, or the shoulders. But when she turned to look at the entryway no one was there but a waiter leaving the room.

She shook her head to clear the strange thoughts, then was startled when the hostess appeared. Reggie couldn't even remember seeing her in the room until that moment. But then again, she'd been having strange, disturbing thoughts.

"Can I get you anything else while you're waiting?" the hostess asked with that smile as she motioned at the champagne and appetizers.

"No, I don't think so," Reggie said.

The smile turned into a slight frown as the hostess looked somewhere around Reggie's shoulder and flicked her hand in that general direction. "Oh, my dear, did you have an accident?"

Reggie glanced where the woman was looking and was startled to see a faint dark stain about the size of a quarter on the blue silk material. It hadn't been there before, and she couldn't remember anything touching her there, except Dennis in the foyer when they'd first gotten here. She brushed at it, but that didn't help. Two dresses ruined in one night?

"The powder room is just down that hallway to the right off the entryway," the hostess said. "The attendant in there might have something that could help take it out before it sets in."

"Thank you," Reggie said as she stood. "I'll be right back." She walked into the foyer, then spotted the hallway.

She crossed to it and went down to the powder room and into a section that looked like a lady's sitting area, complete with a burning fireplace, couches and chairs that framed the hearth, and rich roses and burgundy carpeting. An attendant appeared immediately, a slender woman, quite tall, with auburn hair and dressed in a navy maid's uniform.

"Good evening. My name is Anna. May I be of assistance?"

Reggie motioned toward her shoulder. "I seem to have something on my dress."

Anna got closer and stared hard at it. "What is it?"

"That's just it. I don't know."

"Silk?"

"Excuse me?"

"The dress. Silk, madam?"

"Oh, yes."

Anna walked over to an armoire. She opened it, took something out, then came back to Reggie with a white cloth and a small aerosol can. She sprayed some of the can's contents on the cloth, then gently dabbed at the stain.

Despite the fact tonight had gone wrong on several levels, it was going to be a night to remember. Dennis would come back, and he'd ask her to marry him, and she'd look into his blue eyes ... She swallowed hard. Blue eyes? Ben's eyes? No, gray eyes. Dennis's eyes.

Dennis, who made her feel peaceful, as if she could breathe. Dennis, who as she got to know him was a sanctuary of sorts for her. When Mel had asked her about love, she didn't know why she'd hesitated. Surely this was what love was all about. Not crazy passion. Not tortured souls, the earth moving and rockets going off. But a peacefulness, a quiet companionship that promised a good life. The things she'd wanted all her life. A calm, peaceful man.

Not like Mikey's father. Not like him at all. Not with an intensity that made her breathing tight and her mind begin to shut down. She pushed aside a sudden image of the father, of a man who had a way of looking at her that made her feel he could see past any façade, into her soul. The man's effect on her was so far from calm and peaceful she doubted that any woman could be around him for any length of time. Let his wife deal with it.

That last thought hit her hard. A wife. Of course he had a wife. Mikey's mother. A woman who probably enjoyed the edginess, the disturbing way he had of looking at a person. But that wasn't her. Certainly not her.

"Ah, well, there you go," Anna said as she backed up to study her work. "It's gone, as if it had never been. Poof. Magic."

Reggie crossed to a mirror opposite the fireplace and looked at her shoulder. The stain was gone without leaving a trace. "That's wonderful," she said as she turned. "Thanks so much."

"My pleasure. Just go and enjoy your special evening."

That stopped her for a moment, then she realized that probably anyone coming here was having a special evening. And this was hers. An evening where she'd forget all about emergency calls, ruined dresses, broken pots, a tiny child and a man with blue eyes.

Dennis's entrance into her life had been a total surprise. She had begun to think she never would marry, that all she'd wanted was her own space and peace and quiet. Then suddenly Dennis was offering that life to her.

"Was there anything else I can do for you?" Anna asked.

"No, thanks."

"Then you go and enjoy the best night of your life," the woman said with a smile.

"Yes, I will," Reggie said, then turned to leave.

When she stepped out into the hallway, she never saw him coming.

One minute she was heading back to the table to wait for Dennis, and the next thing she knew, she ran right into a hard, immovable force. For the second time in one day Reggie lost her balance, flailed her arms to try to keep from falling. But nothing could stop her tumble back onto the soft carpeting near the corridor wall.

In the confusion, she heard voices. A man saying, "I'm sorry. I never saw you." And a woman asking, "What on earth happened?"

Then Reggie pressed her hands flat on the plush carpeting, and exhaling in a rush, she looked up, way up, past Levi's, a tweed jacket worn over a banded-collar black shirt, then into deep-blue eyes set in an angular face. A face with a faint scar on a strong chin. A face she recognized immediately, despite the fact the soiled chambray shirt was long gone and no child was present. His hair was slicked back from his face, emphasizing those eyes, eyes she hadn't forgotten.

She blinked as a wave of déjà vu flooded over her, a repeat of the earlier episode in the garden room, down to and including her instant response—the discomfort and awareness that she'd felt under his intense regard. And she wouldn't have been surprised to see the toddler come running down the hallway to tackle his father around the knees at any time.

"You," she breathed.

"Yes, indeed. Me," he said in that disturbing voice as he crouched in front of her.

His eyes were almost level with hers, and the sensations were intensifying, not helped by the way a certain scent of maleness and heat seemed to be infiltrating the air around her.

"And you. A small, small world," he said as he rubbed at one shoulder under the confines of the brown tweed sport coat. "You pack quite a wallop."

"Are you all right?" someone was inquiring over the man's shoulder.

Reggie looked past the man in front of her, expecting to see his wife and find an end to this embarrassing encounter, but the hostess was there, hovering with concern on her face.

"Dear, dear," she was saying, fluttering her hands in front of her ineffectually. "An accident, horrible, horrible," she said, then she looked down at Ben, who was still on his haunches in front of Reggie. "Oh, this is great. I mean, you can help the poor girl. You're a doctor and all."

Ben cast her a glance before returning his gaze to Reggie.

"Oh, you aren't a psychiatrist or a veterinarian or something like that, are you? I mean, you are a people doctor, aren't you?"

"Yes, a people doctor. Little people. I'm a pediatrician."

Reggie gazed back at him. A pediatrician? A kids' doctor with the bluest eyes she'd ever seen, who made her feel as if every nerve in her body had sprung to life...again. An uncomfortable man, and a married one who was looking at her intently. Again. And she didn't like it at all. Not one bit. And she wanted out of there before his wife and kid showed up.

Ben heard the woman babbling behind him, but since the collision, the woman on the floor filled his senses in a way that defied explanation. Her scent, a flowery fragrance that mingled with the heat he'd experienced on contact. Her softness. Even the way she was breathing quickly through her mouth, the way her high breasts tugged at the fine silk of her pale dress. High color touched her finely boned cheeks and amber eyes were wide with either surprise or shock. Probably both.

He hunkered down closer to her, her scent bombarding him, and the urge to lift her to her feet and just hold on to her was startling. The feeling was so strong that it made his little episode in the bathroom seem pale by comparison. He deliberately pressed his hands to his thighs. "Are you okay?" he asked, hearing a strange tightness in his own voice.

She exhaled softly, then started to get up. "I don't need a pediatrician," she whispered.

The huskiness of her voice ran riot over his heightened senses.

"But you need help getting up," he said, then he touched her for the second time. He took her hand, and the action, a totally spontaneous gesture, was probably not the best of ideas. But it happened before he'd thought clearly about any of the sure-to-come ramifications. And the consequences were there in a brilliant flash.

He felt her fingers, the delicate bones, her skin so silky and warm. The way her fingers closed around his. And every atom of his being wanted to do more than just help her to her feet. If he let his needs run rampant, he'd pull her to him, hold her, to feel every curve and angle of her body against his, and he'd...

Someway she was on her feet before he could finish the thought, and just as well, he realized as he stood facing her with less than a couple of feet separating them in the hallway. Her hand was still in his, her eyes wide, and he had to force himself to let her go. It wasn't easy.

Not any easier than it was to stop himself before he reached to brush back the stray tendrils of hair that had come loose from the simple knot. Instead he just watched the way the silky strands fell softly around her delicately flushed face. He pushed his hands behind his back to kill the need that was there just to make more contact with her. He killed that need with the knowledge that the thought had no place in reality. He knew that. He accepted that. But it didn't help when she touched her hair with a faintly unsteady hand.

He took a step back, a self-protective action, then cleared his throat to speak again. "I'm really sorry." He smiled a bit ruefully. "Actually, I seem to be saying that to you a lot, don't I?"

"Yes, it seems so," she murmured as she glanced up at him.

The full impact of her amber gaze made his stomach lurch, but he hoped he kept a neutral expression. After all, he was thirty-five, a sensible person, not some lust-driven adolescent. Even if that was how he'd felt since first meeting her.

"It looks as if your dress survived this time," Ben said as she brushed at the blue silk that did nothing to hide the flare of her hips and the swelling of small, high breasts.

"I'm fine," she reassured him as she looked cautiously past him. "Your son—he isn't here, is he?"

He shook his head. "No, he's probably smashing pots at my place this time.

That almost brought a smile from her, a slight twinkle in her amber eyes, a faint lift of her lips. He'd like to see that smile full-blown one day.

"Thank goodness," she said softly.

"You know each other?" the hostess asked.

Ben never looked away from Reggie. "We've met before, but we haven't been formally introduced."

"His son sort of introduced us," Reggie said quickly.

And Ben knew she would have walked away just like that if the hostess hadn't stopped her with a question.

"Now, why don't you let La Domain make it up to the two of you for this tragedy?"

Ben glanced at the hostess. It was hardly a tragedy. Far from it. Unsettling, intriguing, but not a tragedy.

The hostess didn't stop there. "Why don't you let the establishment buy you both a bottle of champagne?"

Champagne and amber eyes? The idea intrigued him. But the idea of sharing it with her and her date didn't sit well at all. Before he could say anything, the proposal was cut down by Reggie.

"No, thanks," she said.

"But, my dear. You're both waiting, and I thought—" She waved that aside. "Just let me bring you each a drink to your own table, then."

"That . . . that's fine," Reggie said.

Then she was leaving. She was walking away from him to the entryway, her hips moving provocatively and her hand lifting to brush at a stray curl lying against her slender neck. And then she was gone from his sight.

"Dr. Grant? Excuse me?"

He glanced at the hostess. "What?"

"I'll show you to your table now and bring you that complimentary drink."

When he nodded, she headed off and Ben followed her. He should have accepted the drink and had it with Regina, even if her date was sitting between them. But it was too late to do that now. He followed the hostess across the room to the windows, and as she motioned him to his table, he knew it might not be too late after all.

As he slipped into his seat facing the next table, he saw a woman staring out the rain-streaked windows. He saw the sweep of her throat, the ridiculously long lashes lowered slightly over amber eyes, the way a curl lay errantly at her temple. And he saw the empty chair across from her.

The hostess was right beside him, talking to him, and he turned to her. "Excuse me?"

She was holding a cordless phone out to him. "You said you needed to make a call?"

"Oh, yes, thanks," he said.

"I'll bring your drink," she said as she gave him the phone, then left.

Ben dialed home, then sat back and never took his eyes off the next table. Dennis something-or-other was nowhere to be seen, and as Ben spoke to Nancy, he watched the empty seat at the next table. After he found that Mikey was sound asleep and everything was all right, he hung up, and as he put the phone down, the waiter was setting the drink in front of him.

Then the man moved to the next table and placed a drink in front of Regina, and as Ben picked up his glass, amber eyes looked up and saw him. He nodded to her, lifted the glass slightly in her direction. Then, as he took a sip, he made a promise to himself. If the other seat at her table was still empty when his glass was empty, he was going to have his next drink with her.

REGGIE DIDN'T TOUCH her drink. Her nerves were making her stomach feel slightly sick, and it didn't help that the hostess had seated the doctor right by her table. She tried to smile at him, then she looked away and down at the drink in her hands. He was alone.

Waiting, the hostess had said. Wifey wasn't here yet. She stared at the overhead lights dancing in the pale liquid.

She had no idea what the drink was, but she wasn't about to try it now. The champagne had settled oddly in her stomach. The music from the dance area slid around the room, the mellow strains of the sax and the strings a backdrop to the conversations and the sounds of rain and ocean outside.

She turned, not looking directly at the next table and the empty chair there, but glanced out at the night, at phosphorous waves in the distance being dotted by the rain. But no matter how she tried to concentrate on the night outside, she couldn't block out the man sitting just feet from her.

In an attempt to control her thoughts, she concentrated on facts. He was married, had at least one child, and it didn't matter how attractive he was in that rough sort of way. It just didn't matter. It wouldn't matter. He wouldn't be her type even if he were single and childless. Dennis was her type. The man she was going to marry if he asked her tonight. And she wouldn't be sidetracked by strange ideas about any man just because he was uncomfortably male and had a drop-dead smile.

"Excuse me?"

She almost jumped out of her skin at the sound of his voice right by her, as if she'd conjured him up at her side. She turned to find him by her table, his empty drink glass in one hand. "What?"

"I said, I didn't expect this rain."

She stared up at him. "Oh, no. I didn't, either."

He motioned to the empty chair Dennis had left.

"Since you're waiting for someone and I'm waiting for someone, why don't we wait together?"

"I...he won't be too much longer," she said quickly, but that didn't dissuade him one bit.

He simply nodded, then slipped into the chair across from her. "Then I won't be here too long," he said as he put his empty glass down in front of him.

Short of having him thrown out of the chair, she couldn't do a thing to make him leave. So she reached for a celery stick on the appetizer tray, then looked back at him. He sat easily, as if none of the tension in her existed in him. She could almost hate him for that.

"Why don't we do this right?" he asked.

"Do what?"

"Introduce ourselves formally. I'm Benjamin Grant, but most call me 'Ben.'"

She dropped the celery piece on the small plate by her drink and reached for the glass. Holding it with both hands, she didn't lift it. She wasn't sure just how steady her hands would be with him looking at her like that. "Regina Clark."

"Regina," he echoed.

"Actually, 'Reggie.' No one calls me 'Regina' except..." She didn't want to talk to this man about Dennis. "A few people call me 'Regina,' but most call me 'Reggie.'"

"'Reggie.'"

The nickname sounded oddly exotic when he said it that way.

"Well, Reggie, I didn't hear about a storm coming."

He chuckled, a startlingly endearing sound mingling with the music. "Then again, I don't pay much attention to the weather. It just happens, no matter what I know or don't know."

Sort of like him. He just happened. And there was nothing she could do about it. "I guess it does."

"Besides, I'm usually too busy to pay much attention anyway."

She shifted slightly and pushed away the remnants of that soft laughter with the thought that his wife would be here any minute. "I guess your son keeps you pretty busy."

"Oh, he's a handful, okay," he murmured.

She grimaced at the remembrance of her garden room. "That he seems to be."

"I hope there aren't any hard feelings about what Mikey did earlier. I can't tell you how sorry I am that he ruined your plants and..." His gaze flicked over her, then returned to her face. "Your other dress. But Mikey gets panicky if he's closed in. He probably got in your porch room, then couldn't get out."

"He's a little young for claustrophobia, isn't he?"

"He's older than his years," Ben said softly, but there was no laughter in his face now. "But he's really a good kid. A bright child. He knows his colors and recognizes letters and numbers." He stopped himself with a sigh. "I know. I know, I'm not exactly objective where Mikey is concerned. But you know how kids are."

She knew all too well about kids. "How old is your son?"

He took another sip of his drink before saying, "He'll be two just after Thanksgiving."

"He's a very effective two-year-old."

"So, what happened to your friend?" he asked, taking her off guard just a bit by the shift in conversation.

She looked away from him to the rain-streaked windows, and caught his reflection by hers, a man shimmering in the watery windowpanes. She didn't turn to look at the reality of the man. "There was an emergency."

"Medical?"

"No, legal."

"He got arrested?"

Reggie turned back to Ben, her laughter there before she had time to think. Dennis? Arrested? She shook her head with a smile. "No, Dennis didn't get arrested."

"Dennis?"

"Dennis Benning."

"Who is...?"

"A friend."

He tapped his forefinger on the rim of his empty glass. "Well, there are friends and there are *friends.*"

"Dennis is a good friend," she said, not wanting to go into her personal relationships with him.

"A good friend with a legal emergency?"

"Okay, Dennis is a tax attorney, and one of his firm's clients needed his help."

"Oh, I get it. He's a front for the mob and he had to go spring one of them from jail."

The laughter was there again, but she kept it from spilling out too easily as she shook her head. "No, no, no."

He smiled at her, a potent expression that only intensified the tightness in her middle. And she wished he'd be stern and serious, without any of this warmth and teasing.

"Then what?" he asked.

"Okay, Dennis said that one of the firm's most important clients had a tax emergency—not at the jail—and he had the paperwork from the man's file. So, he had to go meet with the man right away. But he'll be back any moment. You must know what it's like having unexpected emergencies, being a doctor and all."

"Oh, yes, I get called away from any number of things all the time." He motioned to the waiter to refill his drink, then looked back at Reggie. "Did you know that house calls are making a comeback?"

She didn't know where that came from. "No, I actually didn't. I'm not sure I've ever had a doctor make a house call."

"You've missed out on a unique experience," he said with a slow smile at the corners of his mouth.

The double meaning hit her hard. A house call from this man? She looked away from him down to her drink, and quickly picked it up and drank half of it, despite the way it burned her throat.

She wondered if Ben's wife was a match for him. Did he make her edgy when he talked or when he looked at her with those eyes? And did he love her passionately and forever? Did he make the earth move and rockets go off for her? For a split second she felt intensely jealous of that unknown woman.

She quickly picked up her drink and finished it in one gulp, hoping against hope that the alcohol would blot out the images and thoughts that almost pounded at her. Things that had no place being here.

But the drink was little defense against what this man across from her could conjure up with just a smile and a word.

Chapter Five

Reggie spoke quickly, saying anything to break her train of thought. "So, it looks like your dinner companion isn't beating a path to this place."

"She'll be here soon," Ben said, and took the fresh drink from the waiter, who had reappeared with refills. "She's been held up a bit."

"Oh, was your wife arrested?" she asked without thinking.

That brought real laughter from him this time, and as the music stopped between songs, the sound of him laughing seemed to fill all the emptiness around them. She wished it had never happened.

"Arrested?" he asked, then shook his head. "No, she wasn't arrested, and she's not my wife."

"Oh," she murmured as any laughter in her died quickly at the idea of his having some sort of tryst at the restaurant. "I see."

"You see what?" he asked.

"That you... I mean, I just assumed you were meeting your wife or she was meeting you." She added quickly as she held up one hand, wanting to stop the discussion she knew could start up, ''But it's none of my business.''

''Actually, you're right. It's not any of your business. But I want you to know that the woman meeting me here is a very wealthy socialite in this city. You probably heard of her, Ruth—''

''No,'' she hurried to say, ''I told you. I don't want to know...about that sort of thing.''

''*That* sort of thing.'' His eyes narrowed, then he took a slow sip of his drink without looking away from her. As he lowered the glass to the table, he said, ''I'm not having some sort of affair, if that's what you think. Far from it. The lady is Ruth Armstrong, an investor—a backer, if you will—for a clinic I'm trying to get off the ground. It's purely business.''

Why should she feel so relieved that he wasn't playing around on some wife at home coping with Mikey? ''A clinic?'' was all she could ask.

''A clinic that I want to set up to help children with specialized problems. It takes a lot of money to be a philanthropist, and Ruth Armstrong has money...and a real bent to help. She asked me to meet her here so she could discuss her part in the project.''

''I'm sorry. I feel so foolish.''

''No problem. But since we're into explanations, why were you and this Dennis person here?''

She fingered her glass. ''We were just having a special evening.''

His eyes narrowed. ''And he's special to you?''

''Yes, he is,'' she said.

"Well, La Domain is the perfect setting for a romantic evening. Too bad it fell through."

"It's not over with. Dennis is coming back and we'll have our evening," she said, then glanced out at the rain and darkness. "I guess your wife will be happy to have you home early if your appointment doesn't make it."

"Actually, no, she won't."

She darted him a look and wondered if there had ever been a man who could demand attention with so few words. "What?"

"She could care less if she ever sees me."

She'd said the wrong thing again, and she hated a habit that had been growing since meeting Ben Grant. "I'm sorry."

"Don't be sorry," he murmured. "There just isn't a wife to care. I'm not married."

He wasn't married? She didn't understand a strange mixture of relief and dread that mingled in her. "I just assumed . . . I mean . . ."

"You do that a lot, don't you?" he said as he slowly traced the rim of his glass with one finger.

"I do what?"

"Assume things."

She could feel her face get warm, and was thankful for the low light in the restaurant. "Well, you have a child, and you seem so . . . so . . ." She searched for a word, any word, that described him, but hated the fact that the only one that came to her was *sexy*.

"Domesticated?" he supplied easily.

That was one word that didn't enter her mind when she looked at him. "No, I assumed..." She bit her lip. "I thought you were married."

"Of course you did," he said as the rain beat softly on the windows, the noise mingling with the music.

Of course she did, and even though she was very wrong, that didn't mean a thing to her. Not when she had Dennis. And Ben had Mikey. A child who had all but destroyed her garden room.

"And I was wrong," she murmured.

"Yes, you were."

"Well," she said on a sigh. "It's just you and the child?"

"Yes, and as you've seen, Mikey makes life interesting."

"I bet he does." She sipped more of her drink, welcoming the warmth that spread in her middle. "Are there any more at home like him?"

"No, but I wish there were," he said.

She stared at him. "Why?"

"Don't sound so surprised. Mikey needs a brother or sister, or maybe a couple of brothers and sisters. Being an only child isn't good for any kid."

She finished her drink and had barely put her glass down, when the waiter was there with a another refill. As she watched the amber liquid being poured into the crystal, she murmured, "Being an only child wouldn't kill someone."

"Oh, you're an only child?"

"No, not even close." She stared at the way the liquid swirled. "But having a lot of kids around isn't an instant recipe for a child's happiness."

"Oh, it's not?"

"Why would it be?" she countered as she glanced up and met his blue gaze.

"It's family. It's roots and sharing and having someone there for you no matter what. Bottom line, you're never alone if there's more just like you at home."

"At least you're right about never being alone." She took a drink, then cradled the fine crystal in her hands. "I bet you think that a lot of kids makes a family—an instant Ozzie-and-Harriet situation."

He laughed again, a sound that made her feel as if he'd touched her. Stupid, she thought as she held more tightly to the goblet. "Didn't old Ozzie and Harriet only have two boys? That's hardly a comparison."

"Okay, how about *Eight Is Enough?*"

"How about *Cheaper by the Dozen?*"

"You want twelve kids?"

"No, and I probably don't want eight. But I'd like a few. Maybe four would be nice."

She couldn't stop staring at him in the soft glow of light from the overhead chandeliers. "Do women you get involved with know this right away?"

He shrugged. "I'm up-front about it."

"And what happens? They run screaming for the hills?"

His laughter showed amusement now, and she hated it. It made her feel as if his essence was surrounding her, seeping into her being.

"I've seldom gotten that far in a relationship."

"Well, you must have gotten a lot farther than that with Mikey's mother."

"Actually, I don't know Mikey's mother."

The man never stopped taking her off balance, and he did it so casually. Saying words in an even tone, while he cradled his drink and looked at her with those blue eyes. "I assume—" She bit off the word and changed what she was going to say to, "I don't understand."

"Simple. Mikey's adopted."

"You and your ex-wife adopted him?

"No, I adopted him as a single parent. I've never been married. How about you? Ever married?"

"No," she said.

"Then there are no children?"

"No, there aren't."

"Then answer me this. What makes you such an authority on the drawbacks of big families?"

"I came from one."

"How many kids?"

"Nine."

He sat forward, getting closer to her across the table. "You're kidding me."

"No, I'm not."

"I've seen a few big families in my practice, but not too many. I had thought the days of large families were long gone."

"Don't tell my parents that," she said as she fingered her glass.

"You're so lucky."

"Excuse me?" she said.

"A family like that. Nine kids." He rolled his glass between the palm of his hands. "That's truly incredible."

She understood that response. He was one of those people who held to the old myth about big families being so wonderful for the kids involved. "I just bet you're an only child, aren't you?" she asked.

"Actually, I don't know if I am or not."

He'd done it again, but it seemed less abrupt this time. Maybe the alcohol was making things easier, or maybe she was just getting used to his way of talking. "Let me get this straight. You don't know if you've got brothers or sisters?"

"No, I don't."

She pressed her hands flat on the table on either side of her glass. There wasn't a trace of humor in his expression, not a hint that he was kidding or making a joke. "How couldn't you know?"

"Because I was left on the steps of a church when I was a week or two old. They never found my parents. Hell, I don't even know what my real birth date is."

That stopped her dead. A child left like an unwanted kitten? She swallowed a bitterness that rose in the back of her throat. "You're serious?"

"Sure," he said in an oddly even voice. "So I don't know if there are more like me out there or not."

The idea of a world with more than one Ben Grant in it came to her. More like him? Thank goodness she didn't know any of them. One was more than enough for her to deal with. "Didn't you ever want to look for them, to see if you could find them?"

"No way I could. I don't even know what my family name is. I got my name from the social worker at the agency where they placed me."

"You were adopted?"

"I wasn't that lucky. By the time the powers that be decided that I was adoptable, I was too old. People wanted babies, not four-year-olds."

She wished she had more to drink, something to fight a niggling sense of pain at the thought of what Ben had probably been through. "So that's why you adopted Mikey?"

He finished his drink, then waved away a refill before he said, "If I tell you why I adopted Mikey, will you promise not to laugh?"

Laughter was so far from her now that she wasn't sure any was left in her. "Of course."

"It's my clock ticking."

"Your clock?"

"You know how women have ticking biological clocks? Well, my clock is ticking, and I decided to do something about it."

She didn't have to think too hard to imagine how he could have quieted his "clock." "That..." She cleared her throat. "That doesn't apply to men," she said, wishing she could take an easy breath around this man.

"Of course it does," he said. "But it's a 'need to be a father' clock in men, not a biological one. Although, I suspect that there might be some biology involved. I've always wanted kids. A family. A big house. Lots of life around me. And when I realized that I was getting older, that if I had kids much later in my life they'd think they had a grandfather, not a father, I decided the time was right, even if there wasn't a wife in sight."

Ben's image in front of her seemed so far removed from anything vaguely resembling a grandfather that she could have almost laughed. "You aren't exactly ancient."

"I'm thirty-five. As it is, I'll be over fifty when Mikey graduates from high school."

She had a flash of this man at fifty, with gray streaking his hair, a few more creases in his face, a look of wisdom in his eyes. Surrounded by kids and loving it. A far cry from where she'd be at fifty. "Fifty isn't that old," she muttered.

"Old enough. That's why now is the time to think about brothers and sisters for Mikey. I actually went and picked up the papers from the agency where I got Mikey, but haven't had the time to complete them."

"You don't have the time to do paperwork, but you've got time to look after another child or three or four...or eight or a dozen?"

"Let's leave it at four. And I'll make the time. A lady who ran one of the foster homes I was in took care of ten kids at once. And she had a saying that time expands to fit more children, just the way love does."

Reggie couldn't stop the snort of laughter at those words. "Oh, did she? And you believed her?"

He leaned closer with his elbows on the table and his fingers pressed together in a tent fashion. His eyes narrowed as he studied her for a long, uncomfortable moment.

"You don't believe that?"

"No, not for a minute. All more children do is consume more time, more space and more energy. There might be love, but even that's stretched pretty thin."

"A cynic, I see," he murmured.

"I'm a realist."

"You felt shortchanged as a child?"

That didn't begin to define what she felt. "Let's put it this way. You don't have a clue what it means to be as much of a mother to my younger brothers and sisters as my mother ever was to them. Or what it is never to have one peaceful moment or a space that's all yours."

"Oh, I think I do. That woman who took in ten kids? One of them was me." He frowned slightly. "I never had a bed of my own until I went to college, and never had my own room until I got my own apartment. I know about short space and taking care of younger kids."

"And you still want the same thing?"

"No, I want my own family. I want kids filling a house that's my home. A family."

He narrowed his eyes on her, their intensity making her breathing catch.

"And what do you want in life?" he asked.

Reggie gazed at the entrance, almost willing Dennis to be there, but the only person around was the hostess, who was looking across at her. The woman waved a hand in greeting, then turned and left.

"Well, just what do you want your life to be?" Ben asked.

She braced herself before she looked back at him, but there was nothing she could do to stop the impact the man had on her. And she could have almost hated him for having that power. He had no right to it. None at all. "Why do you want to know?" she countered.

He cocked his head and studied her for a long, intense moment, then said softly, "Humor me and tell me just what Regina Clark is searching for in this life."

There was no one rushing to her rescue, no Dennis coming back, so she took a deep breath, then said, "I want what most people do."

"Which is?" he prodded.

"Good health, a career that keeps me interested and peace."

He smiled at her. "That sounds like something a contestant for Miss America would say."

His expression shifted to something that made the heat in Reggie flare.

"Not that you couldn't compete with the best of them," he added.

"I don't know what you want me to say."

"Most people say that love is the most important thing."

Then he threw her for a loop.

"So, how's your love life?" he asked.

The heat burned her cheeks and she had to take a steadying breath before she muttered, "None of your business."

He didn't look taken aback at all. "Fair enough. But I've told you about my love life. I thought it was a fair trade-off."

"What you told me is you don't date very much and every woman you date gets informed that you expect to have a ton of kids. That isn't exactly a blow-by-blow description of your love life."

"You know, you're right. I suppose I could give you a—" he raised one eyebrow in her direction "—blow-by-blow description, as you said."

Reggie could barely even think of this man's love life, not when images of him touching, kissing and taking a woman came with such vivid clarity that she literally closed her eyes to try to fight them. But her eyes flew open when she realized the woman with Ben in her mind was her.

Reggie Clark. Damn it, her stomach ached. She took a sip from the water glass before she looked at Ben again.

"Well?" he said. "Is that what you want?"

"No," she replied quickly.

"Okay, then can I ask you something?" he inquired in a low voice.

"I don't know if—"

"One last question, then I'll stop." He made the sign of the cross over his heart. "I promise. Cross my heart."

"What?"

"Does this life you want include kids?"

She sank back in her chair. "No, it doesn't."

"Just like that? No?"

"You asked, and I'm being honest. Some people should be parents, some shouldn't. I shouldn't."

"Why not?"

"I don't want to. I'm being realistic."

"Does being a realist preclude liking children?"

She sighed and wished that the waiter would show up with something, anything, for a diversion. "No, I don't think so. I love my brothers and sisters. But that's it."

"No biological clock ticking?"

Damn it, why did his question have to make her feel so selfish and cold. It wasn't that way at all. But as she answered, she knew how the words sounded. "No. I've been there and done that. I don't want to do it all over again."

"And I'm assuming that this Dennis person agrees with you."

She waved at a passing waiter and asked for another drink, then looked at Ben. "*His* name is Dennis Benning, and he's going to be here soon, so..." She glanced at Ben's empty table. "Where's your rich contributor?"

"I don't have a clue." He didn't look at his table. His eyes never left Reggie's gaze. As he pushed aside his empty glass, he said, "Change of subject, okay?"

She nodded and had barely breathed a sigh of relief, before Ben asked, "Dance?"

"Excuse me?"

"Dance, as in moving your feet in time with your partner's feet and doing it all to music."

"I know what dancing is."

"Then will you dance with me while we wait?" He motioned to the dance floor. "That's great music. It's a shame to waste it."

The last thing she wanted right then was to be closer to Ben, but when he didn't wait for a reply from her, she knew she was in a corner. He stood, came around and held out a hand to her. "Will you dance with me, Regina Clark?"

She ignored his hand. "I...I don't dance very well."

"Neither do I," he said. "So I'll let you lead."

She almost smiled, and just caught herself. "I don't—"

"Come on," he said. "It's a rainy evening and neither one of us has had good luck with our dates. Why not dance?"

She gave up and stood, but didn't take his hand. "Okay, one song," she said.

"Okay," he murmured.

She slipped past him to head for the dance floor. In the domed area, the music seemed to surround her, and as she turned on the hardwood floor, she found Ben right there. He was only inches from her, and without a word, he slipped his hand around her waist with an ease that hinted at an intimacy that shouldn't have been there.

His other hand found her hand, laced her fingers with his, and ever so slowly, he drew her to him. With great effort she managed to keep a slight distance between them as they began to move to the languid strains of "This Magic Moment."

As the drone of the sax mingled with the strings and the music enfolded them, Ben leaned closer to Reggie and whispered, "Relax, I was just kidding about you leading."

She missed her step and stopped for a moment as she looked up at Ben. This close she could see a flare of gold in the irises of his blue eyes, and feel the heat of his breath against her skin. "I... I'm sorry. I told you I wasn't very good at this."

He deliberately drew her closer to him, his hips brushing hers. Her breasts were so close to his chest she could feel each breath he took.

"Lesson number one is to relax and just go where I go," he told her softly.

If she relaxed, she wasn't sure what would happen. She always felt as if she had to be on guard with Ben. But she wasn't quite sure what she was guarding against until he eased her even more tightly against him. The moment she felt the way their bodies melded, how it was to have his length against her, to have the roughness of his tweed jacket against her cheek, she knew exactly what she was guarding against.

And even though she knew she should move back, that she should break the contact while she still could, she didn't. She swayed to the music, closed her eyes and fought every instinct in her to hold on tighter. The man seemed to be everywhere, filling her world, blotting out reason and thoughts. But she kept dancing, fascinated at the way his heart beat against her cheek, the way his hand slipped to the small of her back, its heat almost burning her through the blue silk.

God, she didn't understand any of this. She'd danced with Dennis, but she'd never had the wish to keep dancing forever. Until now. And that scared her. It had to be the drinks mixed with the odd things that had happened, the way Ben seemed to be there every time she turned around. But it wasn't sanity. Not with the music, the rain, the way he held her, that sense of being bound to him that made no sense at all.

"You're definitely a fast learner," he murmured against her hair.

The rumble of his voice startled her, and she lost her step again, but this time didn't try to regroup. She didn't want this to happen. She didn't want to be dancing with this man, someone who wanted twelve kids and probably would go for more if he could. And she didn't want to be doing it when she knew Dennis was coming back and tonight was supposed to be the most memorable evening of her life.

She looked up at Ben, a man who still held her, who gave her barely inches to use as a buffer against the reality of himself.

"Lesson number two," he whispered. "Things happen."

She took an unsteady breath, not about to let "things happen" any longer. She barely recognized her own voice when she asked, "So, do you charge for lessons?"

He was motionless for what seemed a lifetime, before he replied, "Actually..."

Then he leaned toward her, bowing his head to meet hers. And she knew he was going to kiss her. She knew it, and knew how far she'd slipped into insanity when she didn't even try to avoid the moment that his lips found hers.

Chapter Six

Ben knew that the kiss was inevitable—at least the attempt at one—when he first touched her on the dance floor. And when she all but invited it by looking up at him with softly parted lips, he wasn't about to walk away. It had been just moments that he'd been holding her and dancing, but long enough for every fantasy he'd ever had to come to life and center on her. The scent of her, fresh and delicate, the feel of her, slender and warm, and the sense of having looked for her all his life.

When his lips found hers, he knew that whatever search there had been was over. It ended right here, on the dance floor with Reggie. Beckoning lips were a heady aphrodisiac, and when he felt her warm, moist heat, he forgot they were in the middle of a dance floor in the most elegant restaurant in the city.

All he knew was Reggie. Reggie against him. Reggie opening her mouth to his invasion. Reggie filling his senses and his world. And the fact that he hadn't even known she'd existed until just a few hours ago didn't matter. It didn't matter that someone named Dennis was coming for her, that she didn't want kids or that she would probably walk out of here with Dennis. This time was his, and he let the sensations burn into him.

When he realized that the music had stopped, he reluctantly drew back. But looking down into her face, at the faint flush to her cheeks and the seductively lowered lashes, was just about his undoing. If they hadn't been in public, he would have taken her there and then. It was all he could do to find words, even if he said them in a voice that was slightly hoarse. "Paid in full," he whispered.

Her tongue touched her vaguely swollen lips, then she moved back, drawing her hand out of his, and short of refusing to let go of her, he released his hold. Emptiness replaced that sense of completeness, and he stood there like a tongue-tied adolescent. It wasn't until she ducked her head, then walked away from him, that he moved himself.

He followed her back to her table, watched her sink down into her chair, but when he touched the back of the other chair, she spoke abruptly.

"No."

He stopped and looked down at her, but she wasn't looking at him at all. She was staring at the fresh drink in front of her. One of her hands rested on the table, but it was clenched and the knuckles were white. He knew that she was as affected by the kiss as he was, and if she tried to deny it, the way her breasts moved

rapidly with each quick breath she took was a dead
giveaway.

"What?" he asked, without moving.

"Your... your friend is going to be here soon, and
Dennis, he's due here any moment."

"Reggie?"

She wouldn't look at him, but kept staring at the
drink without lifting it. "I'm sorry."

Sorry? He crouched by her chair and reached out to
touch her chin, to try to make her look at him. But
when he touched her, she jerked back. When she finally looked at him, her amber eyes were narrowed, as
if she didn't really want to look at him at all. He drew
his hand back. "What in hell are you sorry about?"

She blinked rapidly, then said, "That never should
have happened. I'm sorry for that."

"Well, I'm not," he admitted bluntly.

"Ben, Dennis is coming and—"

A beeping sound cut off her words, and Ben reached
inside his jacket and took out his beeper. He checked
the readout, saw it was Armstrong's number, then
slipped the device back in his pocket. He exhaled, then
said, "Reggie, I need to make a call. But I'll be right
back. Then we can talk."

"There isn't anything—"

"We'll talk," he said firmly, then stood and glanced
at his table and saw the phone was gone. Quickly he
headed for the entryway to find the hostess. He didn't
want to hear Reggie say anything else, not yet, not
until he could figure out what he was going to say to
her first.

Reggie watched Ben go and took a full breath into her tight lungs for the first time since she'd stepped onto the dance floor. She felt fragmented, her thought processes in such a scramble to find rationality that her heart hurt. This didn't make sense at all. She touched her tongue to her lips, afraid that she'd find Ben's taste there, then reached for the glass to use the drink to wash it away.

She was unnerved to see how unsteady her hand was, so unsteady that she used both hands to lift the glass and take a drink. She swallowed the cool liquid, let it slide down her throat, then put the glass back on the table. But nothing took that sensation away from her lips, not even when she scrubbed the back of her hand across her mouth.

"Damn him," she muttered, and jumped when someone cleared their throat right by her.

She jerked to look to her left, afraid it was Ben there, but she found the hostess hovering over her. "Excuse me?"

"I didn't mean to startle you, Miss Clark." She held out a cordless phone to Reggie. "It's Mr. Benning for you."

"Oh, thanks," she breathed as she took the phone and pressed it to her ear. "Dennis?" she said, closing her eyes tightly. "Where are you?"

She must have sounded desperate, because Dennis asked, "Hey, are you okay?"

"I... I'm fine. I was just getting worried."

"That's nice," he murmured. "And I'm sorry to have to do this to you."

"I don't mind waiting, but I wish you were here right now. That we could dance and—"

"Dance? You dance? The last time we danced, you said you didn't want to do it again."

She swallowed hard. She wanted the memory of dancing to be with Dennis, not with Ben and how he'd wrapped his arms around her. "I . . . I just meant that I miss you."

"I miss you, too." She heard him sigh over the phone. "Regina, I don't know how to tell you this, but I can't get back there tonight."

She felt her heart sink with a sickening thud. "What?"

"This is getting really involved. The client's in a lot of hot water, and it looks as if I'll be here for another hour or two. Would you mind very much if we tried to do this again tomorrow evening?"

She exhaled shakily, then said, "Sure, of course."

"If I get done early enough, I'll drop by to see you. Okay?"

"That's fine," she said.

"Regina, I'm sorry about this. I really wanted to talk with you tonight . . . a night to remember."

If she heard that phrase one more time, she'd scream. "Me, too."

"I'll make it up to you," he said, then he spoke to someone else with him. "I'll be right there to get the file for you." There was a silence, then Dennis was saying, "Regina, the bill is taken care of and the hostess said she'd call you a cab."

"Thanks."

"Regina, I love you."

"Me, too," she whispered, and slowly drew the phone back, then pressed the Off button.

A night to remember. She put the phone facedown on the table, then stood to leave. She'd get out of there, find out where she'd left her sanity, and embrace it with both hands and never let go.

But as she gripped her purse and turned, starting for the foyer to get her coat, she saw her own personal brand of insanity coming back into the room. Ben came down the single step, and he walked right toward her.

She could have run away, or she could have turned and gone off in the opposite direction, but she didn't do either. She stood there and knew this would be closure for her. And she wanted that . . . badly. To end this crazy night once and for all.

He moved closer and stopped. "Were you coming to find me?" he asked with a suggestion of a smile.

"I'm leaving," she managed.

He glanced past her. "Did the mysterious Dennis person come back?"

"Why do you do that?" she muttered.

"Do what?"

"Call him names."

"Names?"

"My Dennis, that Dennis person. Do I need to go on?"

He rocked forward on the balls of his feet, coming perilously close to her, and she made herself stand her ground.

"Reggie, that's not calling names. Calling names would be if I called him a bast—"

"Stop it," she told him. "It doesn't matter. I'm leaving."

"And your escort?"

"He can't get back."

"Too bad," he said, but didn't sound very sorry about it at all. "Thanks for the entertainment."

The damned heat touched her cheeks and she just wanted out of there. "Sure."

"Then I'll see you later?"

She wanted to tell him not if she saw him first, but remembered he'd be next door for as long as he was visiting the Eatons. "Good night," she said, and walked toward the entry.

She paused in the reception area and looked around, then heard someone say, "Miss Clark?" She turned and saw the hostess coming down the side hall, carrying her coat. "I was just bringing this to you."

"Thanks," Reggie said as she took the coat and slipped it on with the hostess's help. As she adjusted the light wool cover, she said, "Mr. Benning mentioned that he took care of the check."

"Oh, yes, he did, and quite generously, too," the hostess said as she stood back and looked at Reggie with a smile.

Reggie wished she knew why the woman was always smiling and looking so satisfied. "He also said that you would get a taxi for me."

"Oh, yes, indeed," she said, and the smile was replaced by a slight frown. "But there is a small problem in that area."

She didn't know if she could deal with any more problems tonight. "What is it?"

"There aren't any cabs available right now. The rain and all. They said there might be up to a two-hour wait for one to come out here. I'm quite sorry."

"Could you call another taxi service?" she asked as she slipped her purse over her shoulder.

"Well, I suppose, but with this rain, I'm sure most will be pretty overextended. I'm just so sorry." She clasped her hands together and smiled again. "I have it. Stay for dinner, and by the time you're done, I'm sure a cab will be available."

There was no way Reggie was going back in there with Ben sitting one table away from her. "I've been snacking on the appetizers. I'm not really hungry."

"You really don't have much of a choice, I don't think. With no cabs and the rain still falling, I…" She waved a hand vaguely. "I just don't see what else there is to do."

Mel might be home, and if she was very lucky, her younger sister would want to drive in the rain. "I'll try to call someone and see if she can come and get me."

"Oh, well, yes, I guess that's a possibility," the hostess said as she turned and picked up the cordless phone from the reception desk. She held it out to Reggie. "Please, be our guest."

Reggie took the phone, turned it on, then dialed Mel's number. Just as it began to ring, there was a crackling sound, then silence. She hit the on button again, listened, then frowned at the phone. "Something's wrong with the phone."

The hostess took it, tried it, then turned and reached behind the desk and lifted the handset of another phone. She listened, then put it back. "The lines are out. Maybe this storm is worse than we thought." She looked at Reggie. "It could be for the best. It just isn't a good night for people to be out . . . unless they have to be."

Reggie wondered if anything else could go wrong tonight. Then she had her answer when someone came up beside her and asked, "Is there a problem?"

She didn't have to turn to her right to know Ben was there. She kept her eyes on the hostess and shook her head. "No, no problem," she said.

"Oh, yes, of course. There aren't any taxis and Miss Clark was going to call someone to come get her, but the phone suddenly went out," the hostess said.

"You didn't get your call through?"

Reggie stared hard at the hostess. "I can wait."

"You don't have to," Ben said.

She literally felt herself bracing when she glanced at him. True-blue eyes pinned her, and a suggestion of a smile played around the corners of his lips. Just as well he didn't smile, she thought, since just looking at his lips did strange things to her. "Excuse me?"

"I've got my car here, and I can give you a ride back to your place."

"Oh, no," she said quickly as she shook her head and clutched her purse to her middle as if it could be

used as protection against this man's effect on her.
"You have to meet Mrs. Armstrong. To get all that
money."

"Ruth Armstrong and her money aren't going to
show up this evening. Something about her polo
ponies and this storm. So I'm leaving."

She couldn't be around him, not when all she could
think of was his mouth on hers and that feeling of
losing complete control. "I appreciate the offer,
but—"

"Then accept it. My car's outside...and it's raining."

He wouldn't let the matter go, and she couldn't even
think clearly with him this close. "I...I..."

"You need a ride now that your Dennis isn't going
to be here to take you back. So why not get home in
my Jeep?"

She wished she could say no, but there wasn't one
convincing argument against her taking the ride, not
one argument that didn't sound neurotic and silly and
emotional. All driven by a kiss on the dance floor.
And the ride wouldn't be too long. Then it would be
over and she could give the Eatons the bill for her dress
and the smashed plants to pass along to Ben.

"Listen, Reggie, if you really don't want a ride, I'm
not going to push you. I just think that I owe you at
least that after the mess Mikey made of your place."
He held up a hand, palm out, to her. "It's up to you."

She forced herself not to touch her tongue to her
lips. "Dr.—"

"Please, I think we know each other well enough for you to call me 'Ben,'" he said softly.

God, her face felt hot, and she knew the hostess was staring at her, probably wondering if she had taken leave of her senses to be fighting a ride in this weather. She drew in a steadying breath, then managed, "I'm sorry. This evening's just been so mixed up. I'd appreciate a ride."

"Good," Ben said. "Then let's get out of here."

As she turned toward the door, she felt him by her side. Before she could reach out to open the barrier, Ben was there, reaching around her, giving her the feeling of being surrounded by his strength, the way she'd felt on the dance floor. And she almost stopped as a vague, unnamed fear gave her a sinking feeling that it would have been better for her to walk home in the pouring rain. But she forced herself to keep going, out into the stormy night with Ben Grant.

ANGELINA WATCHED Ben and Reggie leave and smiled. It looked as if her first instincts about the assignment might have been very wrong. After the kiss on the dance floor, she realized that if she wanted to start a fire between them, all she'd have to do was touch the two of them together.

She chuckled. Not just a fire. An inferno. Even though she could sense Reggie fighting it. The phone by her on the desk rang, and she reached for it without thinking. "La Domain," she said, then wondered what she was doing. She didn't work there.

"Finally. I've been trying to call for ten minutes and the line's been busy. This is Dennis Benning. I need to talk to Miss Clark again right away."

She thought Dennis Benning would have been too busy with his client to try to call back, what with that mess in the files. She heard a car start, then take off from the entrance, and stared at the front doors. "Oh, Mr. Benning, I'm so sorry. You just missed her."

"You managed to get her a taxi?"

"She has a ride, sir."

"I was going to come back and get her, but as long as she's on her way home, I'll just finish up here, then meet her at her house. Thanks—"

"Very well, sir," Angelina said quickly, not wanting Dennis to interrupt what was happening with Reggie and Ben. Not yet. "But I don't really know where she went," she said, treading a very thin line between evasion and lying. Lying was definitely frowned upon, but misleading someone couldn't be considered actual lying.

"She was going someplace else?" he asked.

"I don't know, sir. I never inquired. Was there anything else I can do for you?"

"No, thanks," he said, then hung up.

Angelina dropped the phone on the desk, then almost realigned herself into the Jeep to hear Ben and Reggie's conversation. But she stopped, as she had a thought. She still had loose ends from New Orleans to clear up and in this rain it would take a good twenty minutes to get to Reggie's home.

With a nod, she moved back to headquarters in the blink of an eye. She liked returning herself much better than being dragged back. As she settled in her own space, she looked down at her viewing area and saw Ben driving out of the parking lot with Reggie sitting by him.

It wouldn't hurt for them to talk on the way home and get to know each other a bit better, then she'd carry on with things. She had some plans already in motion.

THEY HAD barely driven out of the parking lot, before Reggie knew she'd been right. She should have walked. The silence that had lasted only a few minutes was making her stomach tighten, and every time Ben moved, she reacted. Nerves just refused to settle in her, and she found that her hands were clenched around the strap of her purse.

She eased her hands open as they drove onto the main street that led toward the hills. The rain was coming down in torrents. The streetlights were blurred glows in the night, and as the lights from oncoming cars flashed through the rain-streaked windshield, she glanced at Ben.

The watery light defined him as if she were seeing him in a dream. The line of his jaw, the way his hair brushed the collar of his jacket, the way he squinted slightly out at the night in front of them. A blurred vision, but that didn't change the fact that he was an unsettling man. As the windshield wipers slapped from side to side, disturbing the light and shadows, she wished Ben would say something, anything, to break the silence. But when he spoke, she knew that the old saying about being careful what you wished for—you might get it—was very true.

"Thanks for the dance," he said in a low voice.

His words made her stomach knot even more, and the mixture of appetizers and alcohol settled uneasily with her. "I told you I wasn't very good at it."

"I wasn't complaining."

He cast her a shadowed look, and she was thankful that she couldn't see his expression clearly. "Far from it."

She shifted in the seat, moving a bit closer to the door, then looked away from Ben as he slowed when they got into the middle of town. She glanced out at the darkness and rain, where streets were beginning to resemble rivers and the cars were few and far between. "This rain's pretty awful, isn't it?" she murmured.

"I said I wanted to talk, but definitely not about the weather," he said.

She closed her eyes tightly. "There isn't anything else to talk about."

"I wouldn't say that."

"Since we pretty much disagree about everything, the weather seems to be the only safe subject."

"Safe is boring," he muttered.

She felt her hands clench again, and deliberately forced her fingers to splay on the leather of her purse. The man was dangerous on many levels. "Safe isn't all bad," she whispered.

"Oh, the old peace-and-quiet-and-sanity defense?" he asked softly.

"You make that sound as if it's wrong to want a life that isn't tipped on end all the time."

"Life isn't simple. It never has been and never will be for any of us." He slowed as he turned onto the road that headed up into the hills. "Look at this evening. It's been far from simple."

She looked at Ben, a dark man exposed by just the low glow of the dash lights. Far from simple. And she hated the feeling. That edginess, that sense that every breath this man took echoed in her. She swallowed hard and said, "Look, I don't know why things happened, but it was a mistake."

He cast her a dark glance. "Was it?"

"Of course it was," she breathed. "We...we hardly know each other. I'm not the type who—"

"Kisses strangers?"

"Exactly."

"Hmm. This is very educational," he murmured.

"Excuse me?"

"I'm learning more and more about you all the time. I've got a feeling that we're very close to not being strangers anymore."

"We've talked, but that hardly makes us...more than acquaintances," she said, her voice sounding a bit tight in her own ears. "You hardly know me."

Ben shot her a quick look, catching the image of her silhouette in the dimness, backed by the rainy night in the hills as they climbed higher toward her house. Hardly knew her? He felt as if he'd known her forever, or at least had been waiting to make contact with her for most of his life.

But fate wasn't exactly favoring him. He didn't miss the way she held herself, that tension in the angle of her head and the set of her shoulders. God knows, he was tense enough himself. Tension that started the moment he'd touched her on the dance floor. Then the kiss. He took a rough breath and tried to talk casually.

"I know you live alone, you've got a friend—a good friend named Dennis—that you're one of nine, that you've looked after kids most of your life and don't want to again, that you're a pretty decent dancer if you concentrate. But there is one thing I don't know."

"What's that?"

"What sort of work do you do?"

"Book restoration."

He wouldn't have been surprised to find out she was just about anything, but something called a book restorer...? "What's that exactly."

"Exactly, I work in a bookstore where they have a specialized service for restoring first editions and rare editions of books. Renewing them, making them perfect again—or as close to perfect as possible."

"And you do that?"

"I rebind and repair leather. I just finished work on an edition of Shakespeare printed in the 1800s. Not exactly irreplaceable, but it had been in the family for generations. I had to completely redo it."

"And you did?"

"You don't have to act interested in this. Most people think it's pretty boring work and you probably do, especially since you're in the business of saving lives."

"I say what I mean," he said. "Sometimes I'm too blunt, but it's better than playing word games." He exhaled harshly, and spoke with that bluntness before he allowed himself to edit his words. "That's why I won't pretend that I didn't kiss you." God, he could still taste her on his lips. "What's the point in pretending it didn't happen?"

"What's the point in talking about it?" she asked in a breathy whisper.

His hands tightened on the steering wheel, partly to keep the car under control on the slick roads and partly so he wouldn't reach across and touch her just to have that sense of her under his hands again. "I know—it was crazy. Actually, I don't usually kiss on the first date," he said. When she sighed, he added quickly, "I'm sorry. I was trying to joke. I'm just trying to see where this is going."

"It's not going anywhere," she declared. "It can't."

Chapter Seven

Ben had never been a quitter. He'd gotten through college, then med school and his internship on his own by never quitting. He'd started his practice from nothing by never quitting. He'd adopted Mikey by never quitting. He'd never quit at anything that had ever been important to him. And he wasn't about to quit on Reggie, no matter what she said.

As he turned onto Echo Drive, he murmured, "Don't be too sure of that."

"I'm very sure that you're building a family as fast as you can, and I've got Dennis."

He slowed, then swung into her driveway and pulled up to the house and the overhang of the wraparound porch to the right of the bungalow. As he stopped by the side stairs, he shifted to turn and look at Reggie, with the motor idling. "You've got Dennis?" he asked, then finished, "but has he got you?"

The rain beat on the roof of the Jeep and streamed down the windows, while the windshield wipers tried to slap it away, and Ben held his breath. He didn't know what he expected from Reggie, but it wasn't for her to stare at him through the shadows and remark, "Dr. Grant, as you've said before, that's none of your business."

"It's not?"

"No." A single word said in a tight, low voice.

"Why not?"

"You don't give up, do you?"

"No."

She gripped her purse as she looked at him through the shadows. "You should."

"Give me one good reason to say good-night and walk away—just one—and I'm out of here."

Ben didn't know what he expected, but it wasn't for her to say, "Mikey."

He felt as though a high he'd been riding since first seeing her was starting to sink. "Oh, the kid thing."

"Yes."

He hated that sense of disappointment, maybe loss, that invaded him, and he found himself speaking with a flippancy he didn't really feel. "Ah, I have a child, therefore, I'm unsuitable." His hold on the steering wheel felt numbing. "Well, that's a blow to the old ego."

"I'm sorry, but . . ."

She shifted farther from him and he could feel the end coming. He hated it.

"Thanks for the ride, Doctor."

He studied her, every line and angle of her face in the shadows, and wondered why it should be so hard to let go of something he never had. "Just an old-fashioned house call," he murmured, then said, "enjoy your life, Reggie, all your peace and quiet and order."

"And you enjoy your dozen children," she said as she opened the door and with a quick "Thanks" plunged out into the storm.

He barely had time to call out, "Four, all I want is four kids," before the door slammed shut behind her.

He watched through the rain as Reggie ran for the house, up the stairs and onto the porch. For a moment as she got out her key from her purse he saw her in the light, and felt a sharp taste of regret on his tongue. He wasn't some schoolboy who fell for any woman who crossed his path. How could a person so diametrically opposed to just about everything he said touch him on so many levels?

As she turned for one brief moment before going inside, she lifted her hand in his direction, and the memory of colliding with her at the restaurant was there. The feel of her softness, that vulnerability he sensed, the warmth of her breath. Then holding her to dance...and the kiss. Then the door closed and she was gone.

He shifted to ease the tightness in his body, and knew he'd been alone too long. He'd been lost in his work to the exclusion of anything else except Mikey. And tonight that was coming back to him full force. Brought home by a woman with amber eyes, a sexy slenderness and a voice that played havoc with any rational thinking. And a woman who "had been there, done that" with kids and probably never wanted to see one again, especially after what Mikey had done to her house earlier.

He felt a smile play at his mouth when he thought of her sitting on the floor in that mess, her hair feathered around her flushed face. A woman who would be right next door when he moved in. Then the smile died. A woman who had a "good" friend, this Dennis person, and hadn't hesitated pointing out that she and Ben were eminently unsuited for each other.

"Damn it all to hell," he muttered as he put the car into reverse to leave. But he didn't go anywhere. The car died suddenly. One minute it was running and the next it was dead. When he turned the key, nothing happened. Not even a click. He sank back in the seat, the only sounds the beating of the rain on the car and his own breathing. Then he glanced to his left, through the rain and night at Reggie's house, and saw a single light come on near a back bay window.

His phone battery was dead. His car was dead. And he had no place to go but inside Reggie's to ask if he could use her phone to call for help. Fate was playing games with him, and he'd just about had enough of them. He hated games.

Reggie quickly went through the darkness to her bedroom at the back of the house. It wasn't until she flipped on the side light by the bed that she realized she was breathing rapidly, almost as if she'd been running in a race. But she knew the source of her tension—the only person who left her with a feeling of being slightly off balance, who had made her wonder if she was slightly mad tonight.

"Ben Grant." She said the name out loud, almost as if it were a test to see what new catastrophe could occur at the mere mention of the man. But there was only the rain on the windows and the sound of her own breathing echoing in her ears.

Quickly she got undressed and out of her damp clothes, then slipped on her gray velour robe against the slight damp chill in the air. As she crossed to the bathroom and grabbed a towel, she said, "Ben Grant."

No thunderclaps or lightning bolts issued from the heavens as she went back into the bedroom. Maybe the evening had been a bad dream. But nothing more. A glitch, a blip. As she loosened her hair, then rubbed the towel over it, she muttered, "An illusion. Ben Grant was just an illusion."

She almost jumped out of her skin when she heard a muffled knocking coming from the front of the house. She stopped toweling her hair and listened, then it was there again. A rapid knocking, then the bell rang. Dennis. He'd come by on his way back to his place. And she needed to see him right then, almost desperately. She draped the towel around her neck, then hurried through the house, switched on a light by the front door and opened the door.

But Dennis wasn't there. It was Ben, with the stormy night at his back and the low glow from the porch lamp showing rain-spiked lashes and water clinging to his darkened hair. And she knew she should have never said his name out loud.

As his eyes flicked over the robe and towel, her bare feet and her damp hair curling stubbornly around her face, she felt a heat against the chill in the air. But this was a heat she didn't welcome.

"My car stalled, and my cell phone's dead. Can I use your phone to call for help?"

She shivered as a chill breeze invaded the house. "It's raining hard, but you got just as drenched coming up here as you would have if you'd run over to the Eatons' house."

"Why would I do that?" he asked.

"You're staying there. I just assumed—" She cut off her own words, not about to start that again. "I mean, your place is so close."

"Well, I'm afraid you don't understand," he said, then looked past her. "But can I come in while I explain? It's cold and wet out here."

She blinked at him, but her instinct to slam the door on him was quickly controlled and she nodded. "I...I guess so." When Ben moved to enter, Reggie jerked back out of his way, not wanting any contact.

As he went past, he brought the dampness of the night, rain and a tinge of heat. She swallowed hard before swinging the door shut and turning to him. He was running his fingers through his damp hair, then he tugged at the front of his jacket, shaking it slightly. The man seemed to fill the front room, and that uneasiness that always came when she was near him crept back again.

"You said you'd explain," she said quickly, and knew it was too quickly when he cast her a narrowed glance.

"The truth is, I don't live at the Eatons' house. They're in Florida, I think."

"But you said you were..." No, he hadn't. She'd assumed it. "I thought you were part of their family, someway."

"I'm not. I was just over there looking at the house." A trickle of water escaped from his hair and ran down his temple. As he swiped at it, he muttered, "I've got to start paying attention to the weather." Then he stripped off his jacket and hooked his finger in the collar to hold it away from him. "Can I put this somewhere until I leave?"

"Just hang it there," she said, and motioned to a wooden peg coatrack on the wall by the door.

He moved over and slipped it on one of the pegs, then turned to her as he raked his fingers through his wet hair and more moisture trickled down his temple. "Would you do me a favor and share that towel?" he asked, pointing to the towel around her neck.

"I... I'll get you a fresh one," she said, for some odd reason not wanting him to use the same towel she did. She turned to hurry into the kitchen and said over her shoulder, "I'll be right back."

By the time she'd retrieved a fresh towel from her bathroom, then headed back into the living room, she saw Ben crouched in front of the stone hearth, touching a match to the carefully stacked logs. Logs she'd searched high and low for, perfect logs that looked just right in the fireplace she'd never used. And never intended to use.

"Ben," she said as she hurried across to him. "The fire—" But her words were uttered at the same time that he dropped the match onto some crumpled paper he'd pushed under the logs.

Then he stood to face her. "I hope you don't mind. It seemed like a fire would be nice on a night like this."

She looked down at the logs that had cost her by the piece, at the way the flames licked around them, then with a hissing and a popping sound caught fire themselves. "Yes, it's nice," she murmured.

"The towel?"

She gazed at the towel in her hand, then held it out to him. "Oh, yes," she said. As he scrubbed the terry cloth over his face, she noticed the way his shoulders tested the material of his black shirt, and where he'd undone the top two buttons, she could see the suggestion of dark chest hair.

She bit her lip and took a step back, looking away from him to the fire in the hearth. "I've never used the fireplace before," she admitted.

"I can't believe that. If I had a fireplace like this, I'd have it on every day." He laughed softly and she stared hard at the dancing flames. "I'd probably turn up the air conditioner just to use the fireplace in the summer. The Eaton house has two fireplaces. They're great. A huge one in the sitting room, large stones and a high hearth."

Reggie realized that Ben had never fully explained about himself and the Eatons. "You said you weren't staying there, but you were over there looking at the house."

"Yes, Mikey and I were looking at the house."

She kept staring at the fire, its heat very welcome through her robe and against her bare legs. "Looking?"

"Yeah, looking. Where's your phone?"

She motioned to the table near the couch. "Over there."

She closed her eyes as he moved behind her, then she heard the sound of dialing.

"Oh, great," he muttered.

She turned to see Ben sitting on the couch, the phone receiver in his hand, and he was frowning at it. "Is something wrong?"

"Busy," he said. "The auto club is never busy, but it's busy now. They must get a lot of calls on a night like this," he added as he dropped the receiver back in the cradle.

"I'm sure you can get through in a few minutes."

He looked up at her as he raked his fingers through his damp hair again, leaving it slightly spiked at the front. "I guess so."

"You were saying about looking at the Eaton house...?"

He appeared blank for a moment, then stood and said, "Oh, yes. We went over there to look at it."

"Just to look at it?"

"I don't mean standing on the street and looking. I mean going through it and looking at it."

The truth suddenly dawned on her. "Oh, no. The Eatons aren't selling, are they? They said they were thinking of it, but were going to wait for a few years, then move to Florida to be with their children."

"Well, they've moved up their timetable a bit, and they're anxious to sell right now."

And Ben was looking at it to buy it. Right next door. And there were no fences, just hedges to define the property lines. There had never been a need to have fences, since there were no children around. Until now. "Oh," she breathed, and moved to the chair closest to the hearth. She sank onto the fire-warmed fabric and hugged herself. "You're thinking of buying it?"

He moved to the fireplace, then crouched and reached for the poker from the brass set she polished but never used. As he jabbed at the logs, sending sparks flying up the chimney, he said, "No, I'm not thinking about it."

Relief was enormous for her, but short-lived.

"I *am* buying it," he added.

She stared at him, at his back, the way she could see the muscles move under his shirt, the strong hand that gripped the poker. Then she started when he looked at her over his shoulder, his eyes hooded.

"So, we're going to be neighbors."

Her hold on herself tightened with each word he said until her fingers felt almost numb. "Neighbors?" she echoed.

He slowly stood, then moved closer to her and looked down at her. She hated the way he had a tendency to always stand over her like that. But if she stood, she would run right into him.

"Yes, neighbors. Is that okay with you?"

"Why shouldn't it be?"

"I don't know, but you seem almost pained by the announcement."

Pained? Stunned would be a better word. "I was just thinking that I'm going to miss the Eatons," she said, finding that partial lie from somewhere.

"Nice people?"

"Very nice. Older, quiet, settled."

"Ah, I understand," he murmured.

She shot him a sharp look. He couldn't understand that she was worried about seeing him day after day, about knowing he was right next door. A most disturbing man. "You do?"

"You're concerned about my future children breaking into your garden room and running amok."

He said the words with the suggestion of a smile, but she wasn't amused. "No, I'm not. I mean, not now I'm not. And I guess that's what fences are for."

"You want me to fence the entire property?"

She wished she knew when Ben was kidding and when he was serious. "No, I didn't say that."

She needed space from him, not this overpowering closeness. Shifting to stand, she saw him move back a bit, and took her chance to get to her feet, then moved closer to the fireplace.

"What *are* you saying?" he asked.

He was so close behind her that she could have sworn she felt the vibration of his words against her back.

She shut her eyes tightly against the flames in front of her and took an unsteady breath. "I just meant that—"

"Strong fences make good neighbors?"

Nothing that mundane, she thought, but nodded. "I guess so."

"Or does it just bother you that I'm going to be living next door, beyond the problem of Mikey and the future Grants?"

The man was indeed blunt, and got right to the heart of the matter. And egotistical. "Why should it?" she hedged.

"That's what I'd like to know," he shot back.

When his hand touched her shoulder, the contact made her jump, and she spun around, coming face-to-face with him, no more than inches from her. Her breathing caught his essence, and the warmth of the fire at her back was no comparison to his heat at her front.

"I give up," he said in a low, rough whisper. "Why should it?"

She touched her tongue to her lips, her thought processes shutting down the way they seemed to every time he got this close to her. And she couldn't even grasp at anger, not with him so near, his presence so overwhelming. "I . . . I don't know," she breathed in a shaky voice.

He studied her, his blue eyes reflecting in their depths the flickering of the flames behind her. "I think I do," he rasped, then touched her again.

He wasn't dancing with her. He wasn't knocking her over accidentally, or even walking with her. He was simply touching her, his hands on her shoulders, his fingers pressing through the soft material of her robe, and in that flashing moment before he drew her close to him, Reggie had the painfully clear thought that the man was touching her soul.

Ben had never been one to wax poetic. But when he saw Reggie standing in front of the fireplace with the dancing flames at her back, haloing her hair, a loose riot of curls, and showing her slender legs silhouetted through her robe, he thought of angels.

But his body certainly wasn't thinking higher thoughts. There was nothing the least bit honorable in his memory of holding her while they danced, feeling her breasts against his chest, his hand against the small of her back. The way her hips brushed his. The smell of her hair, delicate and light. And when her tongue touched her lips, he was lost. He knew it, and he didn't fight it.

He touched her shoulders, soft and delicate, even through the material of her robe, and her amber eyes grew wide. But she didn't move away from him. She didn't move at all. Her lips parted softly, inviting, begging to be kissed. And the need in him for this woman he'd known for only a few hours was beyond reason.

Despite the fact that Reggie realized it was insanity, it was beyond her to stop what was happening. When his lips found hers, the world exploded for her. White-hot passion was there, a sensation that consumed her and a desire that she had never known existed. Equal parts of need and fear mingled in her, and every instinct to run was overridden by every instinct to reach out and hold on to Ben for dear life.

Her hands were pinned between them, pressed to his chest against the raging beat of his heart, and there was a sense of bonding that was overwhelming. Need drove her, an urgency she didn't understand, an obsession that frightened her but that compelled her to open her mouth in invitation. To welcome his invasion and wrap her arms around his neck, straining against his strength.

His lips ravished her, taking her breath away, building a fire in her that flared white hot. It was as if another being had taken her over, a being who wanted to be closer than humanly possible to Ben, to inhale and possess him, to feel him burn her soul. Her fingers tunneled into his thick damp hair, and heat was everywhere.

His deep moan vibrated through her, and his lips burned a path along the sweep of her throat, finding the hollow under her ear. Then he was lifting her, moving back with her, and the next thing she knew, they were on the sofa, tangled in each other's arms and legs, her on her back and him against her, his lips never stopping their pursuit as they built an ache deep inside her being.

When her robe was opened and pushed aside, she didn't know. All she knew was that his hands found her breasts, cupping their weight, his thumbs teasing her nipples until she whimpered against the heat of his chest. The ache grew almost too deep and agonizing to absorb, then his hand moved lower, spanning her diaphragm, pressing against her skin, branding her.

Madness. Lunacy. Craziness. Insanity. The words had no meaning to her; they hovered around the fringes of the glory she was lost in, their meaning there but unreachable right then. She wanted skin-to-skin contact. She tugged at his shirt, freeing it until she had her hands under it, against his chest, feeling the light hair with sleek muscle under it.

But she had barely touched him, before his lips took the place of his hands, tasting her breast, teasing the nipple to a hard nub, and she arched back, giving him access. The ecstasy of his touch was beyond bearing, and the coiled knot deep in her being demanded release. But when she would have begged for more, the door chimes sounded—a harsh dose of stark reality in the madness.

Ben stopped with his hand at the elastic of her panties, and when she opened her eyes, he was over her. His eyes burned as intensely as the passion that coursed through her. But as the knocking persisted, sanity returned with a sickening wrench. She was on the couch, half-naked, making love with a man she hardly knew just because his touch reduced her to acting on her lust.

Heat burned through her at the thought of how close she'd come to betraying everything she wanted in life. Without a word, Ben moved back until he was standing, not bothering even to try to hide the evidence of his own desires. He stood over her, looking down, his eyes taking their time skimming over her nakedness, and she moved quickly. She rolled over and sat up, pulling her robe with her, tugging it around her, and she almost jumped out of her skin when Dennis called out.

"Regina. Are you in there?"

"Dennis," she breathed, avoiding looking directly at Ben. "Oh, my God."

"Tell him to go away," Ben said, his voice rough and intense.

She stood, making very sure not to touch Ben in the process, and ducked her head as she knotted the tie at her waist. "I can't do that," she whispered, miserable with her own embarrassment. "But you—he can't see you here . . . not like this."

Ben hesitated as if he'd argue, then he simply nodded and crossed the room, disappearing into the shadows at the kitchen door. Reggie stood very still, trying to figure out what had just happened. And trying to understand how she could have been so foolish. If Dennis hadn't come . . .

The knocking sounded again, then Dennis called, "Regina? Regina? It's me."

She tied the sash at her waist more tightly, then padded barefoot to the door. With a deep, ragged breath she pulled the door back. Dennis was in the house before she even had time to focus on him, in the living room and talking to her in a quick voice.

"This weather is absolutely horrible," he said. "The streets are flooding, and they're sandbagging down by the cove."

She turned, awkwardly pushed at her loose hair, and tried to understand Dennis. But all she was aware of was Ben in the kitchen, listening, probably watching.

"It took me over an hour to get here from the office," Dennis said.

She looked at him, a man so perfect even now when he was wet, his camel-hair overcoat dark at the shoulders from the rain. Perfect. Even with rain dampening his hair. And the man had been going to ask her to marry him tonight. A man who didn't have a clue that moments ago, she was making love to a stranger. God, her stomach hurt, and impulsively, she went to Dennis and threw her arms around him, holding on for dear life.

Chapter Eight

"Oh, Dennis, I'm so glad to see you," Reggie whispered against the dampness of his coat.

"Regina, is something wrong?"

She closed her eyes tightly. "I was just thinking how dangerous it was for you to come here in this storm, but you did and I'm glad that you're safe."

He held her lightly as he patted her back. "I just wanted to check on you. By the way, whose car is that in your driveway?"

She could barely breathe as she moved back and looked into his gray eyes. "Car?"

"Yes, the one in your driveway. The black Jeep. I thought you had company." He glanced around, then saw the fireplace. "I could see sparks coming out of the chimney, and I knew you would have never started a fire. Not when they make such a mess."

She looked past him at the fire that was starting to die a bit, willing herself to have an answer that made sense. "A neighbor parked it there," she finally said with as much honesty as she could salvage. "It isn't working just right because of the rain."

He believed her, but instead of being relieved, she just felt more horrible at deceiving him. He smiled at her and touched her chin, but his touch was cold from being outside. And she barely covered a shiver that shook her.

"I'm just glad you got home safely," he reiterated.

"You should have phoned, and saved yourself a trip."

"I was calling for over an hour, but I kept getting a no-service message. I was worried."

He bent toward her and dropped a light kiss on her lips, a touch as cool as his fingers on her. She wanted to grab him and kiss him the way she had Ben, to reassure herself that the passion was there with Dennis, too. That she'd made a mistake and had been kissing the wrong man. But with Ben in the next room, she could barely respond to Dennis's kiss.

Then he stood back and slowly withdrew his touch from her chin. "Now that I know you're okay, I guess I should be getting home." He smiled at her. "Unless I can talk you into letting me stay here for the night to keep out of the storm?"

She was horrified at the way she immediately recoiled from the suggestion. "Oh, no. Dennis, I—"

"Hey, I was kidding," he said. "I know better than to think you'd just throw yourself into my arms and go crazy. That's what I like about you. Why I love you."

He touched her cheek, hot now with embarrassment, and the chill in his touch made her tremble.

"I'm so sorry about this evening," he said. "But tomorrow night we'll do it right—no calls, no interruptions and we'll talk. I promise that no client will interfere with things."

"So, is your client going to jail?" she asked, not even aware the teasing question was coming until it was out. Or, when Dennis frowned at her, how jarring it had seemed.

"That's hardly funny, Regina. The man is very important to the firm, and he's not a crook."

There was no laughter at the absurdity of the question, and Reggie wished she didn't remember the laughter with Ben when they had talked about the same thing. "Of course he's not. I'm sorry. That was a bad joke."

"Absolutely," he murmured, then turned and opened the door. He let in the cool dampness of the storm, then he said, "Sleep well, Regina." And he was gone, the door closing behind him.

Reggie heard his car start, and barely covered a gasp when Ben came up behind her and spoke right by her ear.

"Stuffy, stuffy, stuffy," he whispered.

She swung around, hitting Ben in his chest with her elbow, and he stepped back, pressing a hand to his middle. "You scared me to death," she hissed.

He studied her, his hair mussed, his shirt untucked, and the comparison between him and Dennis was startling. Almost as startling as the difference between her reactions to their kisses. She moved a step back, regrouping. "If Dennis had found you here, like that..."

"Don't tell me Dennis would punch me out to protect your virtue," he said with a crooked smile.

If she hadn't been so miserable right then, she would have laughed at the idea of Dennis striking anyone. But she could barely keep eye contact with Ben. "No, he'd never do that."

"I didn't think so."

"You don't know him."

"I can't believe that you do."

"What does that mean?"

"A chaste kiss, a little hug, then he lets you throw him out into the storm."

His smile was there, making her breathing almost impossible.

"Some guy."

And her anger exploded, anger at herself and anger at this man standing in front of her so casually, as if they'd never done more than exchange hellos and goodbyes. "I didn't throw him out."

"He asked you if he could stay."

"You were behind the door. What was I supposed to do? Besides, you told me to get rid of him."

Ben tucked his fingertips in the pockets of his jeans and it was then that she noticed the top snap was undone. God, she'd done that, she thought. And her mouth went dry.

"But he went willingly. What sort of man would give up that easily?"

"The man I'm going to marry," she blurted out.

The words hung between them, and there was no smile on Ben's face now. Just something that could have been labeled shock, then a narrowing of his eyes. "This isn't a joke, is it?"

She shook her head, but didn't say anything. Biting her lip, she moved away from Ben toward the fire. But the warmth was gone and she was suddenly very cold.

"Reggie?"

She didn't turn, but stared at the embers until her eyes ached.

"Reggie?" he said again.

But he was closer, so close his voice seemed to surround her.

She hugged herself and bit her lip...hard. Then she managed to say, "Just go."

"Hey, I'm not Dennis. I'm not leaving like that. Not after—"

Her eyes burned from the smoke from the fire and from ridiculous tears that came from nowhere. "No, don't," she told him shakily. "Don't."

"Don't what?"

"Just let it go, Ben. It was a mistake, a horrible mistake. I don't know what even happened, but it shouldn't have."

"But it did."

"And it doesn't matter," she stated. "You've got your life, and I've got mine."

"And never the twain shall meet?"

She shut her eyes and ignored the tears that silently rolled down her cheeks. "Do you want me to be blunt?"

"What I want is for you to look right at me and tell me that you love that Dennis person."

She took an unsteady breath, but couldn't turn to face him. "I'm going to marry Dennis Benning and I'm sorry, more sorry than I can say, that this happened tonight."

He was silent for so long Reggie thought she was going to be sick. Then she felt him touch her shoulder, and she jerked back, spinning around, ready to run if she had to. But she never got a chance. Ben was there, an immovable barrier to any flight. Then he had her by her shoulders, and he pulled her to him.

In one shattering moment, he kissed her. It was more than a kiss; it was almost as if he had branded her, and the instinct to strike out had barely formed before he pushed her back from him. She was facing him, and the look on his face was edged with real anger.

"Have your life, Regina, with its order and peace and quiet. And forget this ever happened, if you can." Then he turned from her and walked to the door.

"Your—your car, it . . ." she stammered.

He stopped only long enough to grab his jacket and put it on as he said over his shoulder, "Don't worry. I need the fresh air." Then he reached for the door and jerked it open.

She closed her eyes before she saw him actually leave. But she heard the door open, then slam against the night. In the silence that followed, she sank down on the chair by the fireplace, buried her face in her hands and cried. She never cried, but she did now, and didn't even know why.

ANGELINA HATED being zapped. As she caught her breath, she realized that her anger was nothing compared with the look on Miss Victoria's face, when she saw her superior right in front of her.

"Angelina," the woman said, standing for emphasis. "Have you been monitoring the Clark-Grant situation?"

She shook her head. "No, I was finishing up the assignment from New Orleans, and since Ben and Reggie were getting along, I—"

"Getting along?" She bit out the words as she waved her hand at the wall. "Is this getting along?"

Angelina turned to the shimmering screen, then it focused on rain and night and Ben running from Reggie's house. He got in his car, slammed the door, and the screen went inside the car. He pushed the key in the ignition, but the car didn't start.

"Is that your doing?" Miss Victoria asked. "Tampering with his vehicle?"

"No, it's not."

"Humph" came the sound from beside her, then she caught the action of Miss Victoria pointing at the car in the picture a moment before it started.

In a squeal of tires and a muttered oath, Ben backed out onto the rainy street, then drove off into the night.

With a flash they were inside with Reggie, who was in a chair, her face hidden. She was crying. No, not just crying. Sobbing.

"Oh, my goodness," Angelina said.

"This is not a result of your goodness," Miss Victoria declared. "I shudder to think what would have happened if I had not checked in on the proceedings as one of our periodic evaluations of new assignments." She sighed heavily. "A horrible mess."

Angelina wanted to ask what had happened, but she didn't have the nerve. So she echoed, "Yes, horrible."

She watched Reggie stand and grab a towel off the table by the couch, heard her mutter, "Good riddance," then saw her brush at her face with the terry cloth. With a sharp movement, Reggie held it back, stared at it, then with a disgusted sound threw it across the floor. With that, she crossed and locked the door, then turned and started toward the back of the house.

"Forget this ever happened!" Reggie told herself. "It's a nightmare, and it's not real, and Dr. Ben Grant just does not exist. He's an illusion, a horrible apparition."

Angelina almost flinched at the anger in Reggie's voice and was horrified that the seductive couple on the dance floor had ended up like this. It was as if someone had tampered with them and reincarnated them as the Hatfields and McCoys. Now, that had been a horrible mess for everyone concerned.

"Well, Angelina, what are you going to do now that the whole project is in grave danger?"

She wished she knew as she turned back to Miss Victoria. "They were dancing, and they kissed. I just don't see how this could have happened."

"If you had been concentrating on this assignment, none of this could have happened."

"I'm sorry. I'll fix it as soon as possible. Let me take a day or two and figure out a new plan."

"We don't have a day. That young Mr. Benning is going to talk to Regina tomorrow, and as soon as she meets his parents and gets their approval, he's going to ask her to marry him. Whatever you do, it must be done quickly."

"Yes, of course," she murmured. "I'll do my best."

Miss Victoria looked at her with a lifted eyebrow. "We trust that will be good enough."

"Yes, ma'am," she said, and left the office the conventional way, stunned by how humans could mess up the best laid plans. Humans. Now she had to come up with something totally remarkable to fix this mess, and all because two humans could go from wanting each other to hating, with an ease that made her head swim.

BY THE TIME Ben got back home to his condo near the marina, he'd had time to calm down. But no amount of space could block his sense of frustration. Reggie marrying that wooden stick, that jerk who never messed up a fireplace, a cold fish? He remembered the passion in her and cringed at the idea of that idiot extinguishing it forever.

He entered the darkened downstairs, saw no light under the door of the housekeeper's room, then went upstairs. He paused by Mikey's door, listened, then stepped inside the nursery, softly lit by the clown lamp near the changing table. He crossed to the red metal crib and looked down at his son.

Mikey was fast asleep, with his covers balled at the end of the bed. He was sucking on a new pacifier, one with a clown on it. He'd finally given up crying for his favorite pacifier, which Ben hadn't been able to find when they got home. He was on his stomach, his diapered bottom in the air and his lashes making ridiculously long arcs on his cheeks. A great difference from those first weeks when he'd come to live here. There hadn't been nightmares for a while, and no more waking every hour screaming. Mikey looked peaceful now.

Just the sight of the child brought sanity back after a horrible bout of insanity. "Oh, Mikey, I love you," Ben whispered. "When I first got you, I promised that you'd be loved, that you would be the most important thing in my life and that you wouldn't ever be alone again."

As Mikey sighed, squirmed a bit, then settled again, Ben finally saw clearly. Mikey really was everything to him, and no matter how desirable or how beautiful or how fascinating or how sexy Regina Clark was, his son took precedence. And Reggie had made it very clear that she didn't want kids. She'd been there and done that, as she'd said. And if she didn't want Mikey, she didn't belong in his life.

He brushed the cap of blond hair back from Mikey's face, then leaned down and kissed his cheek before he tugged the blankets back over him. Quietly he left the room.

Being a father was a new and strange trip for Ben. He learned things all the time. Tonight he'd learned that loving a child put the rest of his life in perspective. Kids could cut through all the illusions and wishes and get right to the reality.

Ben went into his room, and as he stripped off his clothes, he fought the memory of Reggie tugging at his shirt, of her hands on him. Quickly he went into the bathroom and turned on the water in the shower stall. He didn't bother to wait for the warm water, but he stepped under the cold stream and braced himself as the chill started to banish a heat that came just at the thought of Reggie.

She'd be their neighbor. That made him uneasy, but he pushed that feeling aside. The house was great, perfect for Mikey and any other children who came into their lives. It didn't matter about a neighbor with amber eyes. It didn't matter at all. He reached for the sponge and started scrubbing it over his chest, but there was little he could do to scrub away that feeling of her hands there. Or that persistent wish that Dennis had never shown up.

He stepped out of the shower, grabbed a towel and went into the bedroom. For a moment he looked at the huge bed and wondered if he'd be able to sleep tonight after what had happened. He didn't want to toss and turn, tortured by the images of Reggie.

The phone by the bed rang, and he crossed to answer it. In a few moments he knew that he wouldn't be in the bed after all. He had an emergency at the hospital. As he quickly dressed and went downstairs to leave a note for Nancy, telling her what was happening, he felt a degree of relief to be going back out into the storm. At least he wouldn't have time to think too much about what he'd almost had tonight.

REGGIE AWOKE the next morning to a raging storm outside and the feeling that she hadn't slept at all. The rain beat against the house with a vengeance, shaking the windows with its force and making whistling sounds in the eaves. She shifted, knew immediately that she couldn't go back to sleep, and really didn't want to. Not when that sleep was punctuated with the strangest dreams.

Ben and Dennis, shifting from one to the other. Seeing Dennis and going up to him, then looking up into Ben's face. Kissing Dennis, and having Ben be the one to touch her. Ben walking down the street with kids following him like a mother duck and her ducklings. Funny dreams that left her with no laughter. Fragments of dreams that she couldn't hold to and didn't want to repeat. Dreams that robbed her of her rest and left her more tired when she awoke than when she'd finally fallen asleep.

She pushed herself up. Her eyes felt gritty and her mouth was dry. Even as she sat in the room where the gray light of day crept in, she knew whom to blame for the way she felt. Ben Grant. The man had come into her life less than a day ago and she had more damage in her life to show for his entrance than just broken pots and dirt in her garden room.

She sighed as she pushed her tangled hair back from her face, and grimaced. She had a horrible headache and her head pounded dreadfully, and it didn't help that if she was honest with herself, she'd admit that she was the one who could have stopped the whole debacle. But she hadn't. She'd danced with him, let him kiss her, taken the ride home and allowed her hormones to take over. And she hadn't done a thing to stop the inevitable. Thank goodness Dennis had shown up when he did.

She pushed herself up and scrambled out of bed, the air chilly through the thin cotton of her T-shirt and making her head pound even more. There was none of the warmth that the fire had given last night, and thank goodness, none of the heat that the man had generated. Quickly she crossed to the bathroom, and cringed again when she saw her reflection in the mirror over the old-fashioned pedestal sink.

Her hair was tangled around her face, a face that looked pale and had puffy eyes, with a few traces of mascara still streaking her cheeks. She turned on the hot water and grabbed a facecloth, then scrubbed at the stains. She still didn't understand why she'd cried like that. She hadn't cried for as long as she could remember.

She dropped the facecloth when she heard the doorbell ring. For a moment she didn't move, afraid it was a repeat of last night. Then it rang again and again, her head throbbing almost in time with the noise.

She tossed the cloth down, went back into the bedroom, grabbed her robe and slipped it on as she hurried toward the door. The bell rang again just as she reached for the knob and called out, "Who's there?"

"It's me. Mel."

Just what she needed, and at dawn, too. She braced herself and opened the door. Mel rushed in, almost bowling her over, and as she closed the door she turned to her sister. "What's going on?"

Mel had Reggie's coloring, but with brown eyes, and she was taller, almost five-nine. She took off a bright-yellow raincoat and threw it on the floor by her feet, then stood there in a plaid shirt and black leggings. Looking slender and disgustingly wide-awake, she said, "This rain is something else again. You wouldn't believe all the streets that have flooded. I had to take three detours just to get here, and it took me over half an hour. Can you believe it?" She skimmed off a rain hat and tossed it on top of the dripping raincoat, then shook her head, making her wedge haircut ruffle around her face.

"For heaven's sake," Reggie said as she stooped and picked up the discarded rain gear. "You can't just drop them wherever you want." She crossed and hung the garments on the wooden hooks by the door, ignoring the fact that Ben had hung his coat there just hours ago. She slid a mat under the rain clothes as they dripped, then turned back to Mel. "It's just as easy to hang them up."

"Yes, Mother," Mel said with a small curtsy, then slipped off her black boots one at a time and kicked them vaguely at the mat. Neither one hit their mark.

"Don't do that," Reggie said as she nudged the boots onto the mat with her toes.

"I didn't come here for a lecture," Mel said, her freckled face looking so innocent with no makeup and her hair short and simple. She studied Reggie for a moment, then said, "Boy, you had a rough night, didn't you?"

"Mel—"

She sniffed, then turned and peered in the direction of the hearth. "A fire in the fireplace? That's positive debauchery for you." She looked down the hallway, then back at Reggie. A grin broke out on her face. "Oh, boy, was I wrong. Talk about throwing caution to the wind, acting wild and impulsive." She leaned closer to Reggie and whispered sotto voce, "He's still in there, isn't he?"

Reggie's headache only got worse with the idea that Mel meant Ben, that she knew someway. No, she couldn't. She wasn't talking about him. Reggie wasn't thinking straight. Her sister meant Dennis. "Mel, no one's in there," she said, her teeth almost clenched. "I was quite alone until you showed up."

"I could dream, couldn't I?" Mel asked, then turned and padded in her stocking feet across to the kitchen. "Caffeine, I need caffeine," she said as she disappeared into the other room. Then the lights flashed on there. "Give me caffeine," Mel yelled from the next room.

Reggie went after her. By the time she stepped into the kitchen, her sister already had the water in the coffeemaker and was turning it on.

"There," she said, "My caffeine fix will be ready in minutes." She rested her hips against the counter behind her as she looked at Reggie by the door. "So, Dennis isn't here?"

"No, he's not," Reggie said, then moved to a cupboard by the refrigerator, fished around in it and found a bottle of aspirin. Her head was about ready to explode, and Mel wasn't helping at all. She got a bottle of water out of the refrigerator, then took the aspirin with one gulp of the cool liquid.

"What's wrong?"

"Headache," she muttered as she twisted the cap back on the water bottle and put it back in the refrigerator.

"Dennis gave you a headache? Oh, boy, that doesn't sound too promising."

Reggie turned and glared at Mel. "No, he didn't. I woke up with it."

"But not with him. I should have known that you wouldn't have thrown caution to the wind like that." She laughed. "I know you well enough to know you probably said, 'Yes, Dennis darling, I will marry you,' you drank a toast with herb tea, then he drove you home."

It made Reggie feel slightly nauseated to realize just how wrong her sister was. "Mel, is this why you showed up on my doorstep at dawn—to make bad jokes?"

"I came so you could fill me in on the big night," she said as she got two mugs out of the cabinet by the sink. She set them on the counter by the coffeemaker, then looked back at Reggie. "Okay, tell me how he asked you?"

"He didn't," Reggie said as she sank into one of the chairs by the wicker table in front of the windows.

"What?" Mel stood up straight, eyes wide. "You're kidding?"

"No. He had an emergency and it ruined the whole evening."

"Oh, Reggie, what a bummer."

"Yeah, a bummer," she muttered.

"So, you went home and he went to the rescue of some tax embezzler? Like the Lone Ranger or something?"

"Not even close," she said. "It was just a problem he had to take care of, so I came home. We're going out tonight to try again. He made the reservations and it's all set."

"Well, how spontaneous of Mr. Perfect," Mel said with heavy sarcasm.

"Dennis just wants everything to be—"

"When was the last time he did something with you that's not planned?" She laughed as she picked up the coffeepot, then started to fill the mugs. "I bet when you have sex he calls to arrange it ahead of time. You know, 'Regina, darling, please wear the little black number, and make sure that you have the bed made'?"

"Oh, Mel, that's enough," she said. There was no way she'd tell her sister that she and Dennis weren't sleeping together, that they hadn't yet and had agreed they could wait for a while.

"Reggie, can you really be happy with a man like that?"

Reggie pressed her fingertips to her temples and the throbbing there. Words were there to be said. "Of course I can be happy with Dennis." But an image of Ben came to her with such startling clarity that all she could do was mutter, "I don't want to talk about this."

"What about mad, passionate love? What about wanting someone so desperately that you're almost crazy to have him?"

Mel's words were too close to the reality of the previous night. Way too close. So close that Reggie felt her whole body tense with the memory. "That's lust," she mumbled, "Not love."

"Lust, love—they can both be there together."

Reggie buried her face in her hands and asked, "What makes you such an expert?"

"I'm no expert, but if I ever fall in love, it's going to be like lightning striking and the earth moving, and me knowing that if he doesn't touch me, I'll die."

Reggie swallowed hard. That wasn't true. It couldn't be. Not when Mel was describing the way Ben had made her feel for a fleeting moment in time.

Reggie knew that you didn't have to be in love to

experience any of that. There just had to be a man who burst into your life and turned it on end. Not a man you loved, just a man who made you think of fantasies and dangerous things. A man like Ben Grant.

Chapter Nine

Reggie looked up at Mel and said, "I have to get ready for work. Drink your coffee and see yourself out."

"Wrong," Mel said as she carried two steaming mugs across to the table. She put one in front of Reggie, then took the seat opposite her. "It's Sunday, Reg, and although you work six days a week, you don't go in today. So we can talk as long as we want to."

Reggie couldn't sit there and talk, not when everything Mel said brought last night back with a vengeance. "Melanie, I don't have time."

"Oh, don't call me that. You sound just like Mom when she's mad at me." Mel took a tentative sip of the brew, then frowned. "This needs sugar," she said, and popped up out of her chair to hurry over to the pantry. As she passed the French doors on the back wall, she glanced through the glass, did a double take, then turned to the door. "Reggie, my God, what happened in there?" she asked as she opened the doors and went into the garden room.

Reggie had totally forgotten about the ruin left by Mikey Grant. She put down her coffee and went after Mel. As she went through the doors into the room, she noticed that the rain was letting up, but a real chill was left in its wake. She saw Mel put the table back on its legs, then crouch by the pile of broken pots and the spilled potting soil.

"Reggie, is this what the Eatons' cats did last night?"

"It wasn't cats."

"Then what—"

"The Eatons are selling the house, and the new owner was over looking at it. His son got away from him, got in here and proceeded to demolish all my new plantings."

Mel looked at Reggie over her shoulder. "How old was this one-man demolition crew?"

"About two."

Mel got to her feet and turned with a smile. "A two-year-old next door? I bet you just love that. Let's hope his parents put up a ten-foot wall, for the kid's sake."

"His dad apologized and said he'd pay for everything." Reggie glanced at the mess again and murmured, "The man wants a lot of kids."

"Boy, did he move in next to the wrong person," Mel said as she swiped at her hands, then turned to go back inside. "If I were you, *I'd* put up the fence."

Reggie looked out the rain-drenched screens and could just see the top of the Eatons' house above the hedges that showed the property line. A white, two-story, rambling house, and a dwelling that would soon be Ben's. "Yes, a fence might be a good idea," she murmured, but something in her knew that no fences would protect her from the impact Ben Grant had on her.

As Reggie went back into the kitchen and closed the French doors, she heard someone knocking at the front door. She stood motionless by the sink, listening and dreading another visitor, whoever it was this time. She didn't want to see Dennis and she certainly didn't want to see Ben again. "Well, Reggie, are you going to answer it?"

She shook her head. "No. I...it's probably a salesman."

When the knocking kept going, Mel exhaled and said, "Well, if you won't answer it, I will."

Images of Ben standing there froze her to the spot. "Mel," she called as her sister went to get the door. "I'm not home to anyone."

"Sure," Mel called back.

Reggie crossed to her chair and sank onto it, then took a quick drink of the coffee. The bitter brew trickled down her throat as she heard the door open.

Then Mel was saying brightly, "Good morning."

There was talking, muffled and low, then the door was being closed. She heard Mel coming back into the kitchen, and glanced at her as her sister took the chair across from her again.

"This is for you," Mel said, and tossed a small white envelope onto the glass-topped table between them.

"What is it?"

"That was a real-estate agent, and she's working on the house next door. The man who's buying it, a Dr. Grant, is supposed to be coming by later today, around seven o'clock, to do some measuring. She couldn't contact him—something about an emergency and he's out of reach. But she can't be here, so she asked if you could please give him the key for her."

"No," Reggie said quickly before she could stop the word.

Mel frowned at her. "Hey, I know they've got the kid from hell and all, but she only wanted you to give him a key."

It sounded so rational, but Reggie didn't want to be around Ben again. "I never said he's the kid from hell, not at all."

"Let's call him a discipline-challenged child then, but it won't hurt you to give Dr. and Mrs. Dr. Grant the key. Just drop it and run, if the kid scares you."

"There isn't a Mrs. Dr.," she murmured as she picked up her coffee and sipped it again, but never touched the envelope.

"Oh? A single dad?" Mel leaned closer. "Is he cute?"

"Oh, Mel," Reggie said with a sigh.

"Just asking. I'm not attached right now. And a doctor... Boy, wouldn't Mom be happy with a doctor in the family? So, tell me what he looks like."

Reggie could lie and say she hadn't even noticed, but that was too big a lie even for her. "He's okay." A decided understatement, but safe. "But he wants twelve kids, Mel."

"Eleven more like the kid who tore up your garden room?"

"Yes."

Mel put down her mug with a thud and stood. "So long. I'm outta here. Even I can't deal with someone like that."

"Exactly," said Reggie, sighing again.

Mel motioned to the envelope on the table. "Call the real-estate agent and tell her you can't do it, if you don't want to."

"I don't have a clue what agency's handling the house. I didn't even know it was for sale."

"Then go tape the envelope to the front door and run like hell."

Reggie stared at the white envelope, but left it where it was when she walked Mel to the door.

As her sister slipped on her rain gear, she said, "Now, you call me right after you get home tonight and tell me everything, okay?"

"I'll phone you tomorrow and let you know."

"If I don't get a call tomorrow, I'll assume that you finally did something wild and crazy, like sleeping with the man you're going to marry, and you're all tied up." She grinned lecherously. "Oooh, tied up. Now, that has a nice ring to it."

Reggie couldn't help the heat that touched her cheeks. There was no place in her to joke about any of this. "Mel—"

"I know—none of my business," she said as she put on her hat, then did up her jacket. "If you want to be married to Mr. Perfect, then go for it. And live it up.

Have another fire in the fireplace tonight." With that, she opened the door, then dashed out into the rain with a "See ya."

Reggie closed the door, then turned and leaned back against it. When Ben came for the key, she would be on her way to La Domain with Dennis, where he'd ask her to marry him. Well out of the reach of Ben Grant. So the only thing she could do was tape the key to the door and get out of there unscathed.

Once she made the decision, she felt better. Her head wasn't quite so painful. She exhaled, a deep, cleansing release of breath, and felt okay for a moment. Until she saw the ashes in the fireplace. "Damn it," she muttered, and crossed and began to clean up the remnants of Ben Grant from her life.

BEN HAD BEEN at the hospital until just before daylight. All thoughts of Reggie and what had happened had been pushed aside by the case of a four-year-old who had drunk cleaning supplies. When Ben had finally been satisfied that the child was out of danger, he'd left and come home. He was so tired he could hardly stand, and when he fell into bed he was asleep almost immediately.

As an intern, he'd learned to fall asleep fast, sleep hard and get by with a few hours of shut-eye—a talent that had come in very handy when Mikey had appeared in his life. But this time the sleep wasn't soothing and refreshing. The moment he was under, the dreams came, strange, haunting images, where the only recognizable form was Reggie.

Reggie smiling at him, dancing with him, kissing him, touching him. But nothing he could hold on to until it all solidified into an image of her in front of him, coming toward him, her arms out. He reached for her, held her, relishing the feel of her body against his, wanting her with a desperation that was overwhelming. Need exploded in him, a need that knew no bounds. He felt her, the softness, the curves, then he bent over her to kiss her, to explore her and know her.

Her taste filled him, sweet, inviting, delicious... cherry. Cherry? Reggie? Sleep was gone in that instant, and Ben knew he was on his stomach, his head turned toward an almost painful brightness even through his eyelids. A weight was on the small of his back, and a...a sucker in his mouth.

He opened his eyes just a slit, and with a glare all around, he saw a shadow bending over him. Mikey, jabbing a sucker at his mouth and starting to bounce on his back. The only thought he had at that moment was how thankful he was that he was lying on his stomach. The dreams had left physical evidence of the desire he'd felt, and he stayed on his stomach while he turned his head to evade the jabbing of the sticky candy.

"Good morning, Mikey,". he mumbled. "Where's Nana?"

"'Mornin'," Mikey replied. "Taste, Daddy," he said, and tried to push a sucker in Ben's mouth again. "Taste, taste. Mmmmm. Good."

"Hey, tiger, where did you get a sucker at this time of the morning?" Ben asked as he felt his body relaxing.

"Nana, got more." Mikey began to bounce. "More, more, more."

Ben shifted around until he was on his back and Mikey had fallen to one side. As the boy scrambled to get another position somewhere on Ben's body, he struggled to sit up.

"'Ets pay," Mikey said with excitement as he settled on Ben's legs and waved the sucker at the windows, which were streaked with a light rain. "Go pay."

"No way, tiger. No play today. Daddy has to go to the hospital to check on some patients, and you stay with Nana and make cookies . . . have a nice Sunday inside."

The smile was gone immediately, and Mikey threw himself at Ben, the sucker caught between the two of them. "No go, Daddy. No go."

The child had been all but abandoned by his birth mother, and separation was still terrifying to him. The mess he'd made at Reggie's was proof of that. So Ben was having to work from square one to make him feel secure. "Mikey, Daddy goes away, but he always comes back. Always." He hugged Mikey tightly to him. "I promise you, I'll always come back."

Mikey sighed, then whispered, "I sad."

"Oh, Mikey, don't be sad. When Daddy gets home, we'll go to see our new house, and we'll figure out where to put your swing and slides and tree house and your new room, too.''

Mikey sat back, leaving the sucker stuck to Ben's bare chest. "Wee slide, Daddy. Wee slide!"

"Yes," Ben said as he peeled the sucker off his chest and laid it on the side table. "A wee slide, sure, sport. Two if you want." He cupped Mikey's face in his hands and knew that he'd been right last night. Mikey was the most important thing in his life, and if or when a woman came into the picture, it was "love me, love my son." Very simple.

"Daddy needs to get ready for work, and you need to get some decent food from Nana. Go ask her for a peanut-butter-and-jelly sandwich."

Mikey hesitated, then scrambled off the bed and ran out of the room screaming, "Nana, Nana!"

Ben reached for the phone, put in a call to his exchange, and when there were no message, he threw back the covers and got out of bed to head for the bathroom.

He seldom dreamed, and when he did, it had to be about Reggie. His body started to tighten just at the thought of the dreams, and he walked quickly into the shower and turned on the water. "Rule number one, love me, love my son," he murmured. "So forget about her." Reggie had broken that rule, and that was that.

She had Dennis and her perfect, quiet, childless life, and he had Mikey. Simple. As he stepped under the water, he knew the only thing that wasn't simple was how to forget about Reggie when she was going to be living right next door to them.

REGGIE SPENT most of the day trying to forget about the small envelope still sitting on the table where Mel had left it. She cleaned up the fireplace, then the garden room, and when she found a pacifier with a bear head on it in the rubble, she tossed it on the table by the envelope. When the rain stopped around noon, she headed out to shop for a new dress for the evening.

But when she came back, nothing had changed. The envelope and pacifier were still there, taunting her, not letting her ever forget Ben would be around there at seven o'clock. And she wouldn't be anywhere close by.

As she dressed for the evening in the new dress, a creamy velvet concoction with a deep vee neckline and long fitted sleeves, she knew she had to get rid of the key and pacifier soon. She put the finishing touches on her makeup, then her hair, worn in a French twist with loose tendrils by her ears, and didn't even bother taking one last look before she went into the kitchen to get the envelope and pacifier.

She lifted the envelope; and it was amazingly light to have weighed so heavily on her during the day. But once she had it in her hand along with the pacifier, she didn't look back.

In her low black heels, she knew she couldn't make it across the soaked lawns, so she went out the front door into the chilly evening canopied with a dark, leaden sky. Not taking time to go back for her coat, she hurried down the driveway to the sidewalk and went south to the Eatons' driveway and up the cobbled path to the two-story frame dwelling.

The house was comfortable in its surrounding of elm and oak trees, with sweeping lawns on all sides and a wraparound porch. Part of her admitted that it was a perfect house for Ben and Mikey, with lots of room and lots of character, but another part wished Ben had found a house at the other end of town.

She went up onto the porch, then realized that she'd been in such a hurry to get over here and get this over with that she hadn't brought tape or a tack with which to fasten the envelope and pacifier to the door. She tried to slide the envelope in the crack between the door and the jamb, but it wouldn't fit. Even her attempt to put it under the knocker was unsuccessful. "Damn it all," she muttered as she tried one more time to make it catch by the doorjamb.

She heard a car coming at the same time she sensed light flash behind her. She turned, and the lights pinned her as the car swung into the driveway. And at the same time it started to rain again—a misty haze in the beams of the headlights—she realized Ben had come early. It was his black Jeep pulling up toward the porch and the lights from his vehicle pinning her in their glare as the car swung around at the top of the circular driveway.

There was no escape, so she stood there, envelope in hand, waiting, and hating the way her heart was hammering against her ribs. When the Jeep ground to a stop on the cobbled drive, she made herself not move, and when the door opened, she tried not to react as Ben stepped out into the night. He came around the Jeep, gazed at her for a long moment as he stood in the mist, lean and rugged looking in a denim jacket, Levi's and boots. Then without a word he opened the back door, leaned in, then emerged with Mikey in his arms and a diaper bag over one shoulder.

He ran for the porch, took the steps two at a time, and as she felt the floor move under her feet from his weight, he came up to her. In the faint light of the dying day he studied her, then shifted Mikey to one hip.

"A welcoming committee?" he inquired.

"I just brought this," she said as she held out the pacifier. "And this—"

Before she could tell him about the key, Mikey squealed, "My bow, Daddy. My bow!" and grabbed the pacifier out of her hand.

Ben smiled as the toddler pushed the pacifier into his mouth. "What a lifesaver. We looked all over for that yesterday. He finally took a new one, but this is his favorite bow. He's pretty particular about it."

"Bow?" she asked, the envelope still in her closed hand.

"I don't know where he got the name, but probably because it looks sort of like the shape of a bow. It's one of his many security blankets."

"My bankey, Daddy. My bankey," Mikey said around the pacifier in his mouth.

"No blanket, Mikey. Not now," Ben said, then spoke to Reggie. "Thanks for bringing it over. But how did you know we'd be here now?"

"The real-estate agent said you'd be here at seven."
She held out the envelope. "And she left this for you."

Mikey grabbed the envelope and held it up in front
of him. "Daddy, what dis?"

"Well, it's not another bow," Ben said, without
looking away from Reggie.

"It's a key for the house," Reggie said.

He quirked one eyebrow at her. "What house?"

"This house." Reggie was beginning to think she
had fallen down the rabbit hole where nothing made
sense anymore. "Your new home."

"Open, open," Mikey said, shoving the envelope at
Ben.

"Why do you have a key to this house?" Ben asked
as he warded off Mikey's thrusts.

It amazed Reggie that although the child was
adopted, there was something about father and son
that totally matched. She just didn't know what it was,
but there was something there, a oneness about them
that she didn't understand.

"The real-estate agent couldn't make it and dropped
the key at my place for you to get it. She said she
couldn't get ahold of you all day, and—"

"I've been at the hospital with a child who swallowed cleaning solution," Ben said, his face very grim
now. "I just got out of there and picked up Mikey."
He shook his head. "I don't understand her leaving a
key with you, though," he said.

"You needed to get in, I assume."

"Yes, but..." He shifted Mikey to the other hip,
then used his free hand to reach in his jeans' pocket.

He pulled out a single key. "She gave me one yesterday when we agreed on the purchase, so I could measure and figure out where things will go."

Reggie stared at the key lying in the palm of his hand and swallowed hard. She didn't need to be here at all. She didn't need to be standing here in her white velvet dress, facing Ben and feeling as if she were starting to tip out of control again just being this close to him. "Well, she said—"

"When did you talk to her?" Ben asked as Mikey methodically ripped little pieces off the envelope.

"Actually, I didn't. My sister was over and—"

"You know what, can we do this inside? It's getting cold out here, and Mikey's just getting over the sniffles." At the mention of his name, Mikey stopped tearing the envelope open and took the pacifier out of his mouth to try to put it in Ben's. Ben drew back. "No, thanks, son. No sharing. But you could say thank you to Reggie."

The boy looked at Reggie, then smiled, a wonderfully brilliant expression. "Tanks, Geegee," he said politely, then popped the pacifier back in his mouth.

"You're welcome, Mikey," she said, the need to leave growing more and more urgent with each passing moment. She wanted to be with Dennis, to be at the restaurant and put this all behind her. "I...I have to get going, but—"

Ben held Mikey out a bit from him, sniffed, then said, "I think I've got an emergency." He shifted Mikey to his hip and pushed the key he had in the door lock. "Come on in for a minute," he said. Then, as the door swung back, he eyed Reggie. "I need to ask you something, but Mikey needs to be checked first."

She didn't want to prolong this, not when she could feel her mouth going dry just being this close to the man. "Dennis is coming soon, and—"

Ben peered out into the night. "He's not here now," he said. "And all I need is a few minutes from you." He looked at her intently, his face unreadable. "Please."

Things couldn't get worse in a few minutes. "Sure, I guess so," she murmured.

Reggie jumped when lightning ripped through the heavens and a split second later thunder rolled.

Mikey buried his face in his father's neck and mumbled, "Make go way, Daddy. Peeze."

"I can't do that, but we can get inside away from it," Ben said, then ducked into the house. He flipped on the old-fashioned chandelier in a foyer done in muted shades of rose, with polished hardwood flooring.

Reggie closed the door behind her, then turned to the Eatons' house. Dustcovers had been thrown over all the large furniture in the living room, which she could see to the right through an archway, and the dining room, which was off to the left through a matching arch. Right ahead was the staircase, with dark wood treads and white wooden spindles. Beyond the stairs, she could see the open door to the back kitchen and family-room area.

The house was chilly and damp, but the overhead light cast a warm and soft glow. Reggie had always liked this house, and the few times she'd visited with the Eatons it had been filled with the fragrance of roses and cinnamon and a fire had crackled in the large rock fireplace in the living room.

Now the hearth was empty, the room still, and the house seemed to be waiting. Then Ben put Mikey down and the waiting was over. Mikey ran to the stairs, took two steps, then Ben said, "Mikey, no. Daddy has to change your diaper."

The little boy stopped immediately, then turned and held on to the railing with one hand. "Go play."

"Diapers, then we'll go see your new room."

Right then more lightning struck, and before the rumble of thunder that followed had died out, the toddler's eyes grew wide, his bottom lip began to tremble and the pacifier fell out of his mouth when he screamed. In a flash he darted back down the steps to hurl himself at Ben.

"Hey, kiddo," Ben said as he gathered up his son in a protective hug. "Daddy loves you, and that storm's outside, not in here. You're okay. Now, let me change that diaper."

Reggie retrieved the pacifier and handed it to Ben. He gave it to Mikey, then cradled the boy gently. Reggie couldn't look away from the two of them. She hadn't known him long, but if any man had been born to be a father, it was Ben Grant. And Mikey was one of the luckiest little boys in the world to have a dad like that. A gentle, caring man. Then Ben looked at Reggie with his deep-blue eyes partially hooded by his lashes. And she knew right then that any woman loved by Ben Grant would be one of the luckiest women in the world.

That last thought brought a bitterness to the back of her throat and she turned from the sight of the man. But that didn't stop her from realizing that if life was different, she could care a lot for Ben. But fate was perverse, or maybe it just had more sense than she ever had. It had given her Dennis, and it would give Ben a woman who wanted children as much as he did.

She hugged herself and stared into the dark, empty living room. A woman to share this house, and to share his life, and to share his bed. Images sprang up in her, and she stopped them as soon as they came to her. She wasn't going to think about Ben being in bed with anyone, especially not when she could so easily imagine herself in this man's bed.

"Get a grip, Reggie," she muttered.

Then she jumped when Ben came up behind her and asked, "What?"

"I . . . I . . ." She shrugged, wishing she could shrug off her errant thoughts. "I was just saying that the . . . the fireplace is lovely."

"I think I told you that I love fireplaces," he murmured as he went around her into the room and snapped on an overhead light. "Always have. A great invention. Too bad I don't know who invented them or I'd lobby for a national holiday on his birthday."

She stared at Ben as he went around the draped furniture to a thick nap rug in front of the raised hearth and laid Mikey down on it. She'd never thought much about fireplaces, and now when she did, she thought about...Ben.

She flinched when lightning flashed again and thunder rolled. As Mikey grabbed for his daddy, Reggie could almost feel the static electricity in the air, that jarring sensation of the world being ready to explode.

Her fear must have been written on her face, because Ben glanced at her as he hugged Mikey again. "You're afraid of lightning?"

Mikey sighed and started sucking on his pacifier once more. Reggie could tell he was feeling very safe in his daddy's arms. And for a moment she remembered being there herself, remembered Ben holding her in front of the fire. But she hadn't felt safe at all in his arms. Far from it.

Chapter Ten

"I never liked storms," Reggie admitted, but knew that what she was really afraid of was just being there.

Ben looked away as he eased Mikey back down on the rug, then took off the boy's jacket. As he started to unsnap the leg closings on the green corduroy overalls, he said, "Are they too messy for you?"

She shrugged. "They're just . . . unexpected."

"Most of life is unexpected, Reggie," Ben murmured without looking at her. "Mikey's gone through a lot of unexpected things in his life. So some things scare him."

Like being locked in her garden room and lightning storms. "He's had a hard time?" she asked, wanting a diversion from her thoughts.

"I'll tell you all about it some other time," he said, and Mikey sighed while the pacifier went in and out.

She stayed by the door and from a distance she watched Ben very efficiently change the diaper.

"You've got that down to a science," she said as he put the clean diaper on Mikey.

Without looking up, Ben said, "Practice makes perfect. And boy do I have practice." He glanced at her, and the smile on his lips made her very thankful she had the buffer of distance between them. "I guess you've changed your share of diapers with all those brothers and sisters."

"More than my share," she said. "Tell me something, do you do this all by yourself or do you have live-in help?"

"I do as much as I can myself—I'm trying to give Mikey a sense of security. But I have a wonderful woman who's a combination housekeeper and nanny. She's been indispensable, what with the vagaries of my practice thrown into the mix." He pulled the overalls back on the boy. "Actually, we went through six women before I found her."

"You're a very thorough person."

Ben shook his head. "Mikey's very cautious about new people. She's the only one he even looked at, let alone let hold him."

It seemed hard to believe that the child wouldn't be outgoing with just about anyone. He still had the envelope, much mutilated now, and tossed it back over his head onto the hardwood floor, then grinned at Ben around his pacifier. He said something that was gobbledygook to Reggie, but Ben seemed to understand.

"Yes, you threw it away. Nice toss, though." Ben picked him up and straightened his overall straps. "There you go, champ."

Reggie felt like such an interloper watching Ben and Mikey, an intruder who had no business being there at all. And didn't want to be there. "Ben, I need to go."

"Geegee, no go," Mikey said, and ran around the draped furniture to Reggie.

Before she knew what he was going to do, he had her in a tight hug around her legs. She looked down at the tow-headed toddler, then back at his father.

The smile on Ben's face was unnerving at best—a crinkling of his eyes and a lifting of his lips, crooked, slightly off center. It was as devastating as it had been the first time she'd seen it. He took his time retrieving the envelope with the key in it, then came over to Reggie.

"My son has good taste in women," he murmured.

Reggie automatically stroked Mikey's head, but couldn't look away from his father. "You . . . you said you needed to talk to me?"

Ben bent down and spoke to Mikey. "Hey, champ, can we let go of the pretty lady?"

Mikey didn't let go, but tipped his head back and grinned up at Ben around his pacifier. "Go see wee slide?"

Ben glanced at Reggie. "Not just yet. It's dark out there and wet." He reached in his pocket, took out a matchbox car and held it out to Mikey. "Here, go play with this on the rug." He motioned to the fireplace. "Daddy needs to talk to Reggie."

Mikey immediately spun around, took the car and darted over to the hearth. In moments he was making engine sounds and roads through the thick nap of the rug. Ben watched him for a moment, and the longer he kept silent, the more nervous Reggie got.

Finally she told him, "Ben, you said—"

He turned back to her, his eyes deep blue and narrowed. "Yes, I said I needed to ask you something, didn't I?"

She nodded. "And I have to get going. Dennis will—"

"Be here to pick you up any minute now?"

"Yes," she said tightly, the large house suddenly feeling very close and small with Ben so near her. "What was it you wanted to ask me?"

Ben hadn't had any question in mind when he'd asked Reggie to come in. And when she was about to leave, he'd said anything it took to keep her there just a bit longer.

Maybe it came from the niggling hope that if she was around Mikey a bit, she'd see how easy it was to love him. Mikey obviously liked her, sensed something in her that she tried to hide or deny or ignore. Or maybe not. Maybe he was just kidding himself. But a part of him didn't want to let go so easily. He looked at her in the soft white dress, saw the way the pulse beat nervously in her throat, and he came up with a reason. "Stores."

"Excuse me?"

"Stores—such as where you and this Dennis person shop."

She closed her eyes, her lashes sweeping low for a second, then the amber gaze was on him. "Mrs. Spenser lives at the end of the street and she's nominated herself the official welcome person for the area. She'll be around when you move in and will tell you everything you need to know. She even brings cookies."

He couldn't help a smile at that. "Chocolate chip?"

"No—actually, she brought me persimmon cookies—but I'm sure you could put in your order," she said.

Just a bit of relaxing showed in her face. He liked that. He liked that a lot.

"I don't think Mrs. Spenser is what I was talking about," he said.

She got wary again. "If you need anything, she's the one to talk to."

He could see she was ready to bolt, and something in him knew that if she left, she wouldn't be back. At least, not without Dennis and probably a ring on her finger. A raging need to touch her, just once more, all but suffocated him. "I have to..." He stopped, took a quick look over his shoulder at Mikey, who was sitting on the plush carpet, making a track around the fringe with his car. He looked back at Reggie. He'd told her he was blunt, and now he was playing games. He didn't want to do that now, not with her.

"Listen, Reggie, about last night, I know what you told me, but—"

She moved abruptly. "No, Ben, don't. I have to leave," she whispered, and moved back a step.

The minute she took that step, a wind came up that shook the windows and howled around the house. When she took another step backward, the lights flickered. She stopped and Ben couldn't take his eyes off her. "Reggie, I'm sorry. I just wanted to make some sense out of—"

"No," she said. "I'm leaving."

Even as she said the words, rain started falling with a vengeance, and the wind drove rain against the windowpanes. He heard Mikey behind him say, "Daddy?"

He held a hand out at his side. "Come here, Mikey. Come to Daddy." Then he spoke to Reggie. "You can't go out in that storm." Ben felt Mikey put his hand in his and he held it tightly. "You'll ruin another dress if you do."

He saw the uncertainty in her eyes.

Then she said, "I'll call Dennis to pick me up here." She turned away from him and moved across the foyer to the phone on an old-fashioned chest by the staircase.

Another brilliant flash of lightning ripped through the night, and the thunder rolled ominously. Mikey almost climbed Ben's leg to get into his arms, and Reggie froze for a moment. As Ben picked Mikey up and held him to his chest, he watched her reach for the phone. The lights flickered again as she picked up the receiver. When she put it to her ear, then jiggled the disconnect buttons, he knew what was going on even before she turned to him.

"It's dead," she said.

She looked trapped, and it hurt Ben to think she wanted to escape so desperately. Despite the fact that he wanted to keep her here forever, he found himself saying, "I have a cell phone. You know, doctors can't be without a phone."

She exhaled, her eyes slightly narrowed. "A cell phone?"

Mikey cringed when lightning flashed again and buried his head in Ben's neck. "You can call that Den—you can call Dennis on it," he said over the rumble of thunder.

"Thanks." She didn't come any closer, but held out a hand.

"It's in the car." He heard the rain coming down in torrents. "I'll go get it, but..." He motioned to Mikey. "Could you hold him for me while I go out?" He found the ability to joke a bit, even though he had the strangest feeling he was helping someone very special walk out of his life. "He's clean, so your dress is safe."

"Sure, of course," she said, and came closer.

"Mikey, go to Reggie for a minute while Daddy runs out to the car." Ben expected a protest, even some crying and clinging, but he was shocked when Mikey twisted and held his arms out to Reggie.

When Ben handed his son to her, he took a moment to watch her take him, then cradle him in her arms. She patted the boy's back and shifted to get him comfortably situated against her shoulder. Damn it, it looked good, too good, he thought, and couldn't resist saying, "You're a natural," before he turned from the sight of his son in her arms. Quickly he headed for the front door.

"BEN, Ben, Ben," Angelina muttered. The man was noble, just too noble for his own good. Getting the phone for her. Did he think this was all a coincidence—the rain, the storm, Reggie being within arm's reach for him? What did the man need, a hit on the head or a giant miracle to get him to take advantage of his position?

She watched as he reached for the door, then knew that she needed to do something. Anything to give him and Reggie a chance to see what was right in front of them. As he reached for the door handle, she waved a hand and wished that humans would at least cooperate sometimes.

AS BEN TOUCHED the door handle, a clap of thunder rocked the air. The lights in the house flickered, then went out completely. A strange silence followed for a moment, then all hell broke loose. In total darkness, thunder crashed, Mikey screamed and the wind battered the house with sheets of rain.

Then somewhere out of the darkness, above the storm and the crying, Ben heard another sound. A soft voice, talking and cajoling, saying things would be all right, not to be afraid, that he was just fine. It was Reggie, crooning to Mikey, but her voice touched Ben in a way he couldn't begin to define. And it affected Mikey, too. His crying changed to a sobbing sound that was muffled and low.

Ben couldn't move at first, then he tried to break whatever spell was starting to possess him, woven by the sound of her voice in the darkness. But he couldn't quite shake off the feelings, not when they over-lapped with memories of lonely nights in the past, times when he wanted someone, needed someone to be there for him. But there never had been anyone that special. Until now. Now she was here, in the dark, holding his son and comforting him, and he felt a gut-wrenching sensation at the realization that he never would have her.

"Mikey, it's okay," he finally managed to say, rais-ing his voice to be heard over the sounds of the storm. He glanced out the side windows by the door and saw no lights at all out there. "The lights are gone," he said as he turned back to the darkness in front of him.

"I could find the fuse box, I think," Reggie mur-mured.

Ben realized that Mikey was quiet, even though it was still thundering outside. "I don't think that would help," he said, going toward her voice in the dark-ness.

"These house have fuses, Ben, and I—"

"It's not just this house. The whole street's out. As the old saying goes, 'It was a dark and stormy night,' with the emphasis on both 'dark' and 'stormy.'"

"There aren't any lights at all?"

He was close enough that he sensed her in front of him, and as his eyes adjusted, he could almost see the shadow of her a few feet away. "Not even street-lights," he said, and heard Mikey sigh. "Is he okay?"

She shifted, then spoke so softly he almost lost her words.

"I can't believe it, but I think he's gone to sleep."

"You're kidding." His voice dropped as he heard Mikey's even breathing. Then he reached out in front of him, felt something soft, and realized that he was touching Reggie's arm. She touched his hand with hers and guided it to Mikey's back. He felt even breathing, then Reggie let go of his hand, and he skimmed his touch up to the boy's face. His eyes were closed and the pacifier was going in and out at a steady rate. "I can't believe it. You worked magic."

"I just held him," she said.

He wanted to say that the magic was her, but he kept that to himself. "Then thanks for holding him," he said as he patted his son's back.

"Sure," she whispered.

He moved his hand down, touched Reggie's arm and felt her tense slightly at the contact. He hated that response to his touch, when just the feel of her made his whole body respond in a much different way. But he made himself touch her again, then cup her elbow.

"Let me get you and Mikey in the living room, then I'll find a light and get the phone." He felt with his free hand in front of him, then eased her forward with him until he felt the doorjamb. Slowly he led her into the living room, found the couch and let go of her to tug the dustcover off. He let it fall on the floor, then touched her again.

God, it was all he could do not to put an arm around her shoulders, to hold her against his side, but he didn't. "The couch. It's right here," he said, then guided her around it and helped her down onto it.

"Do you want to lay Mikey on the couch?" he asked as he stood back, not able to stand inhaling her sweetness any longer.

"No, this is okay for now." He heard her shiver slightly. "Just go find a flashlight or something."

"Sure, but I think I'll start a fire first. It's getting pretty chilly, and the fire could give me some light, too." Ben hesitated, needing the reassurance of feeling her one more time. But he didn't have that luxury. Someone named Dennis Benning did. And that thought made him move away from her. He turned, felt the growing chill in the air, then saw the shadows of the hearth.

"I was looking at the fireplace yesterday, and they've got wood in a storage cupboard." He moved to the right and groped in front of him. "Yes, here it is," he said as he felt the door inset in the stone face of the hearth. He opened it and felt logs, some kindling and folded newspapers. To one side he found a jar of matches. "We're all set," he said as he took a match out and struck it across the stones.

It hissed to life, and he grabbed some logs and fixings, then put them in the grate. When the match started to burn his fingers, he flicked it into the fireplace, and the last flicker of flame caught at a piece of newspaper he couldn't remember putting in with the logs.

The flaming paper flared up, immediately catching the dry wood. He stood, looking at the fire he wasn't quite sure how he'd started, then turned and saw Reggie in the flickering glow from the growing fire.

His chest tightened. She was cradling Mikey on her shoulder, and the fire played highlights in her hair and shadowed her face. He'd never seen anything more beautiful, and it was almost physically painful for him to see her like that.

He had to swallow hard before he could speak. "I'll be right back," he said, and went past her out of the room into the darkness.

He'd find the light, get the phone and stop this right here. It was getting harder and harder on him to think of that moment when she'd leave. And the longer he was around Reggie, he realized that if things went much farther, he wouldn't be able to be gallant and wish her well as she walked off into the sunset with Dennis. *Get the phone and get out,* he thought as he cut through the foyer and started down the hallway to the kitchen.

He passed a shadowy doorway to his left, a small guest bathroom in the entryway, and as he approached the kitchen door, he started having trouble seeing in the darkness. Suddenly he saw the white flash of lightning, then thunder rumbled as if it were in the house with them.

Reggie sat on the couch, felt the warmth of the fire as it caught more, starting to ward off the chill and dampness from the storm outside. She held Mikey and tried to not think about Ben. She tried to forget the image of him in front of the growing fire, the strength in him, the gentleness mingling with it. "Just forget it," she whispered as she closed her eyes. "Just forget everything."

Mikey sighed and snuggled closer to her. A sensation of peace was almost there for her. It was odd how a sleeping child in one's arms could make everything feel better. It could almost make her feel peaceful. If Ben hadn't been so close by. But just as that comforting realization formed, everything shifted.

Lightning flashed across the sky, filling the room with a white glare, then came rumbling in its wake. The next instant, Mikey bolted upright and let out a scream that tore at her heart. She tried to pull him back, to soothe him, but he fought her like a caged animal fighting containment.

"Ben, Ben. Help!" she called as she tried to catch at the frantic child, to stop him flailing his arms and pushing with his feet to get away from her.

He was there instantly, reaching for Mikey, forcing the child against him, wrapping his arms around him and holding him tightly. "Mikey, it's me. It's Daddy. It's okay. It's okay."

Reggie stared at Ben as he paced back and forth, talking constantly, hugging the boy, and she could feel her heart pounding against her chest. She sat on the edge of the couch, her breathing rapid, then finally the child seemed to sag against Ben. The sound of his pacifier being sucked got louder. When Ben eased to a stop in front of the fireplace, he kept jiggling Mikey in his arms.

"Hey, champ, it's okay, it's okay," he murmured, and Reggie heard Mikey sigh deeply before he started sucking on the pacifier again. The firelight framed Ben and the child, and Reggie felt as if she were always looking up at him. And at a distinct disadvantage every time, feeling overwhelmed by his physical presence and by the sight of him cradling a child in his arms.

She looked away from him to her hands in her lap, and couldn't help but marvel at the perversity of fate. Dennis, a man who was perfect for her, never made her feel so aware of everything, so touched by life and so uneasy with the possibilities. Yet Ben, a man who wasn't right for her at all, made her feel that she was sensing life for the first time on a lot of levels.

When Ben came over and sank onto the couch by her, she leaned toward the corner to keep some semblance of a safe space between them. "I don't know what happened," she murmured. "He was asleep one minute and the next, he was screaming."

"Mikey has bad dreams," Ben uttered in a partial whisper as the toddler shifted a bit, then settled. "Bad dreams."

"He seemed terrified."

"He is." Ben patted his son's back and stared at the fire. The pattern of the flames flickered over his face, cutting deep, dark shadows at his cheeks and throat. "He has these dreams, and I never know when they'll come." He sighed. "I don't even know what they're about. He's too young to tell me, but it has to be something from his past."

She felt an ache in her for Mikey, and for Ben, too, trying to deal with him. "What sort of background did he have when you got him?"

"Sketchy. His father isn't known. His mother's gone. All the agency knew when he was put in the system was he'd been handed over to the state. That he'd been neglected. He was basically healthy, but afraid to be touched, afraid of being locked in, afraid of sudden noises, loud voices."

"He was abused?" she asked, unable to think of why any person could hurt a child, any child.

"Probably, in one way or another. I've never let myself think of what could have been. I just try to head off things when they come up and let him know that he's not alone, that I love him."

Mikey stirred anew, lifted his head, then with a deep sigh settled again. "He's pretty lucky," she murmured, thinking that anyone Ben Grant loved would be more than lucky.

"I'm the lucky one. I've wanted kids for a long time, then Mikey came along and suddenly I've got this little life who depends on me for everything. When I get home from the hospital or from a horrible day trying to get a clinic started, he's happy to see me." He slanted her a glance, intent, yet shadowed by the flickering fire. "Your father must have been overwhelmed when he went home and had nine kids happy to see him."

She looked away from Ben to the flames as the logs burned and the rain beat against the windows. "Dad worked two jobs for as long as I can remember, and when he got home, most of us were asleep."

"Your parents love you, don't they?" he asked, taking her aback a bit.

She looked back at him, and found him watching her steadily. "Of course they do."

"But?" he prodded.

"But nothing. They love me. They love all my brothers and sisters."

"How many of each?"

"Excuse me?"

"Boys and girls. How many of each?"

"Five boys, four girls, ages twenty-nine to ten."

"And you're the second eldest?"

"Yes, and the eldest girl."

"So why do you think you don't want to have children?"

She blinked at him. His questions were scattered, yet they found their target with surprising ease. "I just don't," she said, and hated the touch of uncertainty in her statement. And she hated the way Ben could make her have to think about what she wanted and didn't want. "I decided that a long time ago."

"When?"

"When I got old enough to realize that I'd been a mother to at least seven of my siblings, and I'd had enough of it." She clasped her hands more tightly on her lap. "When I realized that my parents never had enough time for us, let alone for themselves. I mean, they love each other. They still act like they do. But they get a minute here, an hour there, and I think that marriage should be for two people. They've always had so many other people involved in it that it's never been about just the two of them."

"And they're bothered by that?"

"No, I...I don't think they care," she said, and stood, needing to move and get away from Ben.

But his voice followed her as she neared the hearth and felt the heat at her front.

"So, you think they don't have a good marriage?"

"No, I didn't say that. Maybe that's what they wanted in marriage. I don't know," she said, and hugged herself. "They never told me what they wanted."

"What do you want in marriage with this...with Dennis?"

She almost said she didn't know, that all her carefully sorted-out thoughts on the subject were being shattered by a man with blue eyes and a child who touched her heart, despite everything. "I want what he can offer me," she said, and was stunned at how shallow that sounded.

"What does he offer you?"

"The life I want," she said.

"A life that you don't have to share with anyone but him?"

"I didn't say that."

"Well, you shared your parents with all your brothers and sisters, and maybe you just want one person to be all yours without anyone else cutting in. To be just two people, without kids taking away from that."

She turned, and saw that Ben had rested his head against the back of the sofa, his eyes hooded, yet she could feel them on her. Damn him, but he had probably hit the nail on the head. If she was honest, she could admit that if there had been any way she could have been part of Ben's life, she'd want him wholly and completely.

That thought shook her, and she had no idea where it came from. But it was there and real. She'd actually thought about being part of his life. A foolish, stupid thought. As he stretched his legs out in front of him, she knew no woman would ever have him totally, least of all her. And she swallowed hard, fighting a sense of loss that was as close to lunacy as anything she'd ever felt in her life. She couldn't lose what she didn't have, and never would.

Chapter Eleven

Reggie tried to regroup as she muttered, "I thought you were a pediatrician, not a psychiatrist."

"Just stating the obvious."

She shrugged, not wanting Ben to understand anything about her. "I need to contact Dennis," she said. But knew that what she needed even more was not to be here with Ben. "Tonight was supposed to be—"

"A night for just the two of you, wasn't it? And you got stuck here." Rain shook the windows and Ben shifted a bit, then eased to a sitting position. "I'll go get the phone."

She wasn't sure she was up to holding Mikey again, not when each time she touched the child, she felt that she was linking with the father. She was saved by Ben's offer.

"I can put Mikey down in there," he said. He motioned with his head to his left, and Reggie glanced at a door that was slightly ajar.

"The Eatons redid a sitting room for their grandchildren when they visited. There's still a portable crib in there.'' He got slowly to his feet. "I can put Mikey down, then I can hear him if he wakes again."

She stayed where she was and made the offer she didn't want to make, but knew she should. "I . . . I could hold him while you go out for the phone."

"No, thanks. It's just easier to put him down."

The memory of his nightmare haunted her. "But if he has another dream—"

"I'll hear him. He gets so restless when he sleeps it's hard to hold him for very long." He started across to the door. "Can you get the door for me?" he asked.

Reggie hurried to open the door, then stood back as Ben carefully went into the dark room beyond. The fire cast just enough light to discern outlines, and she could see Ben move toward one wall, then heard him talking softly.

"It's okay, son. It's okay," he said, then made soft shushing sounds.

In a moment he was coming back toward her, and she faced him with just inches separating them in the flickering light. "I'll go get the phone, then you can get in touch with your Dennis."

Unexpectedly he reached out and tapped her chin, and she froze when his finger lingered there.

"Don't look so worried. You'll call him. He'll ride up on his white charger and sweep you away into the night."

He trailed his finger up to her bottom lip, then the contact was gone.

"A damn lucky man to have you waiting for him every night," he whispered, then turned and headed into the shadows and away from her. "Listen for Mikey, and I'll be right back."

Reggie leaned back against the doorjamb and put her arms around herself. Damn the man. One touch and she felt as if her legs couldn't hold her up. She heard the front door open and close, and she hated it that a person she'd known for twenty-four hours could make her so aware of himself that she sensed only emptiness when he wasn't there.

She moved back to the fireplace, picked up the poker and nudged at the logs, making them flame up a bit more. As heat waves touched her, she stared into the fire and wondered when her life had been turned upside down. But she knew. The minute she'd seen Mikey, and the next moment when Ben had come to rescue him. A knight on a white horse, she thought, and felt her chest tighten.

ANGELINA WATCHED for a few moments, then smiled. So far, so good. Shutting them up together with the child was working. She could sense Reggie's uncertainty, her confusion, and a little upset didn't hurt the process. Ben certainly was drawn to Reggie, despite the fact he was acting noble by running through the rain to get the phone for her. But noble is as noble does. And Angelina was not going to let that nobility cause problems. Not when Reggie and Ben were there, and Dennis Benning was at his house alone, trying to reach Reggie by phone.

She watched Ben run through the downpour, get into the Jeep and grab the cell phone out of the center console. As he flipped it open, Angelina lifted her hand. But she stopped when he hesitated, then closed it and tossed it back on the passenger seat. A surprise, but a very nice touch, she thought with a smile. Sneaky, but it showed he had the right instincts after all.

He grabbed a flashlight from the glove compartment and ran back to the house. As he took the porch steps in one long stride and headed for the door, Angelina withdrew. No one was going anywhere for a while. She'd learned about assuming anything with Reggie and Ben. But as Ben went through the door, soaking wet, with the flashlight in his hand and no phone, she felt a degree of self-satisfaction. Miss Victoria would approve.

BEN HAD LET a degree of fantasy live, with Reggie so close, the fire going, Mikey sleeping. For a flashing moment he'd let himself slip into the fantasy of this being his life. Then he'd been shaken from it rudely by the reminder that there was a Dennis out there in the big, wet world and Reggie was waiting for him, not Ben.

That's when he'd been noble. She wanted Dennis. She wanted the life he offered, and she wanted to be with him tonight. So he'd gone for the phone, through pouring rain, getting soaked in the process. But at the last minute he'd done something totally out of character for him. He hated games, but as he'd tossed the phone back on the console, he'd committed himself to one.

He'd decided right then that he wasn't going to fight fate or help Reggie escape just yet. Whatever happened happened, and he was going to take every moment with Reggie he could get tonight. Mikey liked her, and Ben knew that she liked his son, despite her ideas about children. No one who hated kids could have quieted Mikey the way she had, so naturally, so gently.

As he ran back toward the house, he let a final thought soothe his conscience for leaving the phone out in the Jeep. Reggie wasn't married to Dennis... not yet.

Reggie heard the door open and close, then footsteps, and Ben was there in the doorway to the living room. In the flickering light from the fire, she could see he was very wet. He looked across at her, then held out a dark thing in his hand.

"The good news is, I found a flashlight."

She started toward him, but stopped at his next words.

"But the bad news is, my phone's dead." He tossed the flashlight onto a nearby chair, then raked his fingers through his wet hair. "I forgot to recharge the phone after last night. I'm sorry."

She stared at him, not sure she was seeing things that sprang from fantasies in her mind, or if Ben was really starting to undress:

"I'm soaked, and these clothes are freezing," he said as he undid his shirt, then slipped it off.

If it was a fantasy, it was one that was making her mouth go dry and her heart start to race.

"The phone..." she murmured and had to swallow to finish. "It won't work?"

"Not at all," he said as he balled his shirt up and used it to roughly dry his hair. Then he looked at her, the flickering light showing his hair spiked at the front, his eyes totally unreadable. "Sorry. I've never done that before. I've got a dozen charged batteries at home, but forgot to change batteries last night. And today's been pretty hectic. Besides, if the phones are out here, they're probably out where Dennis is anyway."

When he touched the front of his belt, Reggie blurted out, "No, don't...I mean..."

"Oh, you assumed that I was going to take off my pants, didn't you?" he asked in a low voice.

"No, I just..."

"Assumed that I was going to strip." He laughed softly. "It has potential, but I wasn't. I was going to take my beeper off my belt." He unsnapped a small black thing from his belt, then crossed the room to the couch and sank onto it. He laid the beeper on the side table as he looked up at Reggie by the fire. "Besides, the pants can't come off with these boots on."

As Ben methodically began to take off his boots, the storm was lost on her. She barely heard it over the pounding of her heart and while she dealt with the tightness in her chest.

"Did Mikey stir while I was out there?" he asked as he dropped one boot to the side, then started on the other one.

"No." She touched her tongue to her dry lips. "No, he's been quiet."

"Great," he said as he put the other boot to one side, then tugged at his socks. "The longer he sleeps, the better it is." He gazed up at Reggie with shadowed eyes and tossed the socks after the boots. "Goodness knows how long we're going to have to wait for this storm to run its course."

When he stood, Reggie had a vision of him with his chest naked, the sprinkling of dark hair like an arrow disappearing into his waistband. She turned so quickly from the sight that she almost stumbled on the hearth, then reached for the door to the wood storage. *Do something,* she told herself, *and get ahold of yourself.*" She had to keep busy and figure out just how to deal with this. And pray for Dennis to show up of his own volition. A white knight to rescue her, she thought, a knight to rescue her from Ben Grant.

She took out two logs, but before she could toss them into the dying fire, he was there. He reached around her, his chest against her back and shoulders, and he took one of the logs from her hand.

"Let me do that," he murmured.

And she let the other log drop to the hearth with a thud.

Turning away from him, she went back to the couch and sat down. She steeled herself, then looked at Ben. A sigh of relief was there before she could stop it. He was still in his jeans. Any thoughts of seeing him standing there naked seemed as foolish as they were disturbing. He put the logs on the fire, maneuvered them with the poker, and she watched the way his muscles rippled on his back with each movement.

It was stupid. There were any number of men who were in shape, who looked this good without a shirt. Dennis. He took care of himself, working out at the gym, eating a low-fat diet, not drinking much alcohol, never smoking. But a treacherous part of her admitted that he didn't look like this. As Ben stood and stared into the building fire, Reggie admitted that he had a wiriness about him that didn't come from measured exercise.

She didn't realize how lost she was in her thoughts until he turned. It startled her when he faced her, his fingertips tucked into the pockets of his jeans. "That'll keep us warm," he said. "At least for now."

She looked away, was embarrassed when she tried to talk and stammered. "What—what about—about Mikey? Do you thinks he's okay? I mean, that he's not too cold in there?"

"Mikey's fine," he said.

"I wouldn't...I mean, you said he had a bit of a cold and..." She had to stop herself from lacing and unlacing her fingers in her lap. "It's so damp."

Ben crossed to where Reggie was sitting and sank down by her. She stared at her hands, aware of him settling just inches from her, and as he thrust his bare feet out toward the fire, she had the silliest thought. The man even had nice-looking feet. Strong, large feet. And for the life of her, she couldn't remember what Dennis's feet looked like. Maybe she'd never seen them. No, that wasn't right. She had. Of course she had.

She didn't realize she had sighed until Ben asked in a low voice, "So what was that sigh for?"

"What sigh?" she inquired as she looked at the fire leaping to new life.

"The heavy sigh. Are you worried about your Dennis? I wouldn't be if I were you."

She sat forward, resting her elbows on her knees and cupping her face in her hands as she studied the flames. "Why wouldn't you worry?" she asked. "It's a tornado out there."

"It's not a tornado, but even if it were, your Dennis wouldn't be out in it. He seems like an eminently sensible man who wouldn't take off into a raging storm to wander the streets in search of anything or anybody."

That almost made her laugh. Almost. "No, he wouldn't."

"And, as I said, he is eminently sensible. So he's someplace warm and dry, waiting this out, and if the electricity is out and the phones are out, he probably assumes that you're doing the same."

He was right, but he sounded so smug saying it. "If *I* were eminently sensible, I'd be in my own home waiting this out," she muttered. But she wasn't eminently sensible about anything anymore.

"You were doing a good deed. Don't be too hard on yourself. Besides, this isn't too bad, is it?"

It was a disaster. "It isn't what I planned."

"It isn't what I planned, either, but we can't do anything about it."

She watched one of the logs fall to the back of the grate and shoot sparks up the chimney. "I guess not."

"And the thunder and lightning seem to be over. That's good. And we've got a fire. That's good. And Mikey's asleep. That's very good." He shifted a bit lower on the cushions. "Life isn't all bad," he said with a sigh. "I love fires. Some of the best memories of my life involve a fire in the hearth."

She didn't know if he meant it, but his words brought back the night before with a vengeance. The fire; the heat; Ben touching her, kissing her. She stood abruptly and moved away from him to the hearth. She wished she could laugh this all off, that she didn't feel his eyes burning into her, that every movement by Ben didn't cause her whole being to tighten.

She hated feeling helpless, but that's just what she felt at the moment. Then, to make matters worse, tears of frustration quietly slipped down her cheeks. She mumbled, "Damn it all" as she swiped angrily at them.

"Hey," Ben said.

She knew he was getting up, that he was right behind her, and when he touched her on her shoulders, she almost expected it. But it didn't lessen the effect his touch had on her. God, he could have branded her and had it be less a permanent feeling. "It's—okay, it really is. Trust me. We'll get through this just fine."

Oddly, she did trust him. It was herself she didn't trust at all. Not when her impulse was to walk into his arms. "I . . . I'm fine. It's just . . ."

He gently turned her around until she was facing him, mimicking his actions of the night before. Then Reggie looked up at Ben and felt as if she might have won the skirmish last night, but she surely hadn't won the war. Not when her hands seemed to lift of their own accord and touch his bare chest. She felt his breath catch at her touch. Sensations of heat and muscle and springy hair were there, shooting through her fingertips. And his heartbeat echoed in her, racing wildly.

As he narrowed his eyes, he slowly framed her face with his hands. His thumbs eased away the tears on her cheeks. The fire flickered over his face, and she knew that no man had touched her like this. Ever. But why did it have to be Ben? Why did it have to be now? Here? And why didn't it surprise her at all?

"Oh, God, what's happening to me?" she asked. "I never cry." She took a shuddering breath. "And now . . ."

"And now?" he repeated, his eyes trailing over her face, then resting on her lips.

Reggie stood very still, knowing what was going to happen and feeling as though she'd been waiting for it forever. This wasn't reality. This wasn't her or her life, but a glitch in time. A space where reality could just slip away. And right then, she didn't want reality. She wanted this. Ben close, his heart beating under her hands and reality kept at bay.

He closed his eyes for a long moment, and his touch on her trembled, then his lips found hers, and Reggie turned her back on everything and everyone but Ben and here and now.

She felt his lips tentatively touch hers, then his tongue gently demand admission, and she felt something in her fall. A barrier, common sense—she didn't know what. But it was gone, and she lifted her arms to encircle his neck and draw him closer to her.

She felt his shuddering response, then the kiss turned to a possession. It stopped just being contact and went into a world where it was all new and ready to be explored. His taste filled her, and the feeling of his body against hers was a heady sensation. It drove her on, building a fire in her that didn't compare with the one in the hearth. It licked around her, heating her to the boiling point, and with every touch, every taste, it grew higher and higher.

She arched toward Ben, welcoming his kisses, which rained down on her eyes, her ears, then her throat, and when he groaned—a low, animalistic sound—she trembled. He wanted her and she wanted him. It seemed so simple. So right. And when she felt the world start to tremble, she thought it was thunder again, but there was no sound, no storm outside, just inside herself.

"Oh, Ben," she breathed, burying her face in his chest.

His hands were on her, and she felt her zipper glide down, then the white velvet was slipping away. His hands were on her shoulders, then spanning her bare rib cage. The velvet fell lower, until she felt it around her ankles. In one movement she lifted her foot and nudged it off her feet and away from her.

In her panties and bra, she clung to Ben, and when he eased her back and down onto the plush carpet by the hearth, she went willingly. They were together, stretched out on the nappy fabric, and Ben was over her. When she opened her eyes, she saw him so close to her, the light from the flickering flames playing over his face. His hand touched her cheek, his fingers a feathery contact as he traced the line of her chin, then touched her parted lips.

"God, you're beautiful," he murmured in a raspy whisper.

She felt as if her world had stopped, that this moment was the only reality in the eye of a storm. As his finger smoothed her bottom lip, she trembled, then found herself echoing his touch, her fingers brushing the strength of his jaw, then finding the incredible softness of his lower lip. She felt him take a sharp breath, then his tongue touched her finger.

"Oh, man," he whispered, "I never knew that fireplaces could be this great, or I would have had one in every room I've ever been in."

If she could have laughed, she would have. But when she tried to, the only sound was a whimper. His hand on her shifted, finding her breasts through the lace of her bra. Her eyes fluttered shut as she arched to his touch, welcoming it. When the snap of her bra gave way, Ben tugged the garment free of her.

Then his hands found her breasts, and an ache deep in her grew with frightening speed, engulfing her, melding with a need for the man that knew no bounds. He came closer, then his mouth took the place of his hands on her breasts, teasing her nipple with his tongue, tugging at a cord in her that felt ready to snap.

She moaned softly, her whole being centered on the spots where his body touched hers. His hand skimmed over her stomach, then found the elastic of her panties. For a brief moment, she felt everything stop, the world grind to a halt, then she touched the silky fabric and pushed it downward. Ben did the rest, and the panties were gone.

When he touched her center, she gasped, arching suddenly, and when he pressed the palm of his hand against her, she cried out. With agonizing slowness, he started to make circular movements against her, building a frenzy in her that threatened to consume her. Higher and higher she climbed, spiraling upward into the unknown, then suddenly there was nothing.

"Oh, no," she gasped as she opened her eyes, then saw Ben was standing, taking off his jeans, then jockey shorts, which were white and stark against his dark skin. And she could see the evidence of what he felt, and as he removed the white cotton she held out her hands to him. "Please," she whispered, the word ominously like a plea on her part.

He didn't move for what seemed an eternity, just stood there looking down at her, his gaze almost as potent as his touch. "God, you're beautiful," he said, "more beautiful than I thought possible. I've never..."

His voice trailed off, then he turned and crouched by his pants. He fumbled in the pockets, then he was back with her, and raised himself on one elbow to look down at her. He didn't touch her. "Are you sure?" he whispered. "Here and now? God knows I want you, but if you want it all—dancing, music, diamonds...?"

"Diamonds?" she murmured with a shaky smile.

"Anything you want," he whispered back.

All she wanted was him, with a single-mindedness that took her breath away. "I want..." she started to say, but her voice was growing shakier with each passing moment, and she couldn't finish. She swallowed, then managed, "Please."

He dropped a quick, fierce kiss on her lips, then moved back and held up a package to her, a tiny foil-wrapped square. His voice was unsteady as he handed it to her and murmured, "I'd never do anything to hurt you."

Tears filled her eyes again, tears that came out of a sense of disbelief that any man could be like Ben Grant, gentle, concerned, and more desirable than any man had a right to be. As he undid the package and fitted it, she wondered when this dream would end for her.

But she didn't want an answer to that. Not when he was here for her. She shifted, pressing herself against him, and lowered her hand to touch him. He gasped, his body trembled, then he was kissing her and exploring her with his hands. Any fire up to now was a mere shadow of the flame that his touch brought at that moment.

The need appeared suddenly and completely, and she knew that all she wanted was to feel him inside her. To know what that was like. And she drew him to her, then over her. She lifted her hips, inviting him, and she felt her breathing catch when he touched her tentatively; then, with exquisite slowness, he filled her, until she knew she couldn't take any more.

Her hips lifted to meet him, and as he began to move inside her, she rocked her hips to his rhythm. There was no gentle building of sensations, but a white-hot agony that seemed to possess her. And as their movements got faster and faster, she clung to Ben, her fingers digging into his shoulders as she held on for dear life.

And when she thought she couldn't take it any longer, that the ecstasy was going to shatter her, she heard Ben cry out, then her own voice mingled with his. For that moment, a single heartbeat, she knew she'd become a part of Ben in a way she had never been with another man. Then everything was lost in the pure sensations of release and gratification. And Ben.

She cried out, over and over again, then felt herself being engulfed by him, sheltered in his arms, lying with him, and before she drifted off to sleep, she allowed only a tinge of regret that this would be all she'd know of Ben.

ANGELINA WAS ZAPPED before she knew what was happening, and when she found herself in front of Miss Victoria, she had a raging headache. One of these days she'd invent something that warned workers when they were going to be taken so they'd be ready when it happened. Not like this. She touched her head, then looked at Miss Victoria.

"Ma'am, what's wrong?"

"We are not impressed by your tactics, Angelina."

She frowned as she pressed her fingers to her right temple. "Excuse me, ma'am?"

"A storm like that is not what we meant when we told you we expected you to do your best. When one has to resort to fooling with nature to achieve an objective, it shows a limited range of abilities."

"But, ma'am, Reggie and Ben—"

Miss Victoria waved at the wall and the screen started to materialize. "Yes, Regina and—"

"No, ma'am," Angelina said quickly as the images started to take shape. "You can't."

"We can," Miss Victoria said as she turned to the screen. With a startled gasp, she covered her mouth with her hand as the solidifying images of Ben and Reggie on the fluffy carpet in front of the fireplace filled the wall. Together, holding each other, naked.

She clapped her hands quickly, and the images dissolved. "Oh, my," she murmured as she pressed a hand to her ample bosom this time. "We had no idea . . ."

"Ma'am, that's why I was in my place." Angelina stood a bit straighter. "Rule number seven is to give all subjects due privacy. One does not want to become a voyeur, does one?''

Miss Victoria narrowed her eyes on Angelina, but the color was still high in her round cheeks. "No, one certainly doesn't. We..." She exhaled. "Since the subjects are amiably situated, the use of the storm is going to be overlooked." She shook her head. "To be perfectly honest with you, we were a bit skeptical about your ability to do this, but one should never prejudge one, should one?"

"You didn't think I could do this?" Angelina asked.

Miss Victoria smiled slightly and waved a hand dismissively. "What does that matter now? We are very pleased. Just make sure that all loose ends are secured, then report back here with a prediction for the future of the relationship."

"Yes, ma'am," Angelina said.

"And Angelina?"

"Yes, ma'am?"

"Enough is enough."

"Yes, ma'am."

"The storm is over."

Angelina smiled. "Yes, the storm is over."

Chapter Twelve

Reggie awoke to near darkness and the heat of Ben all around her, a barrier to the chill as the fire died lower and lower. She stayed very still, taking in the sensations of his heart beating against her back, his arm around her waist, his leg heavy over her thighs. The only sounds were the hiss of the fire and his breathing near her ear. The storm was gone, or it had settled into a gentle rain.

Reggie stayed very still, afraid to move in case the world shifted back into anything that resembled reality. She wasn't ready for that. Not yet. Just a few moments longer with Ben; that's all she wanted. That's all she knew she'd have. Ben deserved so much more than her in his life. He deserved a woman who would give him everything he wanted, everything he needed, even if that turned out to be twelve kids. He deserved the best.

She stared hard at her white dress, abandoned on the floor along with her underwear, which was tangled with Ben's Levi's. So intimate, so revealing. God, she felt an ache in her middle. Nothing would ever be the same again. Nothing. The white dress she'd bought to wear when Dennis proposed to her was the dress she'd worn when she gave herself to Ben. Life had taken a sharp detour and it was all changed. Irrevocably.

She didn't know if she could still marry Dennis, but she knew that she had to leave Ben. She couldn't pretend that she was right for him, but she needed just one more touch, one more kiss, one more memory to take with her. She shivered slightly, and Ben whispered by her ear, his breath warm against her skin, "Cold?"

She closed her eyes tightly, then moved until she was facing Ben on the soft carpet. His arm still rested on her waist and his legs twined with hers. Then he shifted as she opened her eyes, and he raised himself on one elbow to look down at her. His hand slowly came up from her waist, skimming over her breasts, and he smiled slightly when she trembled at the contact.

"Do you want me to put more logs on the fire?" he asked as his fingers found her nipples and teased them with aching leisure.

She inhaled sharply at the contact, then touched him. She pressed the tip of her forefinger to the hollow at his throat, to the wildly beating pulse there, inhaling the feeling as if she could absorb him into her with the simple action. But that was as much a fantasy as thinking that this could be more than now. More than the moment. This man was made to be loved, both him and his son.

Her breath caught, but this time with a simple thought. She could love him in an instant. No, she realized as she slowly drew back and closed her hand into a fist on his chest. She did love him. And it hurt. It hurt like hell. She wasn't anything he needed or deserved. But she loved him.

Her eyes burned and she could barely breathe. "Ben..." she whispered.

His hand moved up to brush her hair back from her face, then his palm cupped her chin.

"Oh, Reggie. I had a feeling all evening that something was conspiring to get us here, to get us together."

His chuckle was a rumble that she felt along the length of her body.

"I don't even understand what's happened." He dropped a quick kiss on her lips, then edged back. "We need to—"

She caressed his lips with her fingers, hating the unsteadiness in her touch. "No, please," she said tremulously. "Don't. Just... just kiss me again," she managed.

When he bent to kiss her, she wrapped her arms around his neck and pulled him down to her. Her kiss was deep and desperate, a wild need to taste and remember, to burn him into her soul. And this time the passion was there without any foreplay, without any exploration. It was just there, white-hot and devastating, driving Reggie to hold to Ben and offer herself to him one more time.

One more time. The words rang over and over in her mind. One more time. And she loved him. God help her, but she loved him. And this was the last time she'd be with him. The last time she'd feel him surround her, and the last time she'd join with him in complete surrender. Because when she walked away from this, she wasn't going to look back. She couldn't. For Ben's sake and for Mikey's, also.

The fires grew higher and higher in her, her need for him all-consuming, then in one easy movement he shifted, spanned her waist with his hands, and she was over him. Sliding down, feeling him, then being filled slowly and completely, as if she'd been made for this very thing. Then she was connected so intimately with Ben that she cried.

As he began to move, rocking faster and faster, the tears came, but the fire grew. Reggie threw back her head, letting the feelings take over, becoming her, allowing the growing ecstasy to fill her completely. And when she knew she was at the edge, that she just had one step more before she was hurled into a space where only she and Ben existed, she cried out. Somewhere she heard her name called, Ben saying it over and over again, then the world shattered into a million fragments of ecstasy that knew no bounds.

For one fleeting moment, Reggie knew a pure pleasure that came from one source. Ben. Then she could feel it slipping away. She could sense that it was going, that she'd never have it again, and the tears burned her cheeks. She collapsed onto him, then rolled with him onto their sides, and as he left her, she felt a grief that overlaid the lingering shards of ecstasy, and she buried her face in his chest.

Ben held her while she sobbed, then gradually the tears stopped. She held to him tightly, letting him stroke her hair, letting him whisper to her, words she couldn't understand, yet needed the way a thirsty man needed water. And as she let herself drift, she felt him kiss her hair and murmur, "Thank you."

His soft voice banished any thoughts of just staying close for a while. She couldn't. If she did, she was afraid she'd do something eminently foolish and stay even longer. So long that getting away would be impossible. And she couldn't do that to Ben. He had his dreams and she wasn't part of them. She couldn't be.

She eased away from him, and a chill quickly gripped her. A chill and a painful embarrassment at her nakedness—a feeling she hadn't had until that moment. She felt his hand hold her for a moment longer, then let her go, and she sat up and reached for her clothes. She grabbed them, then got to her feet and started to walk away.

"Reggie?"

Ben's voice followed her, but she didn't stop or look back. She saw the flashlight where he'd tossed it on the chair, and picked it up. It flashed on, and she used it to go to the entryway. "I'll...I'll be right back," she managed as she played the light down the hall and spotted the guest bath beyond the staircase.

"Hurry," she heard him say as she started down the cold hall, then she stepped into the small room and closed the door. With her clothes and the flashlight clutched to her breasts, she leaned back against the cold wood of the door. There was no heat here, and no tears. Her eyes were burning now, but painfully dry. She was beyond tears. She knew what she had to do, and she knew why she had to do it.

She loved Ben Grant. She'd known the man for twenty-four hours, and she loved him with a passion that seemed unreal. But she couldn't be with him any longer.

Reggie let the clothes fall to the floor, then stepped over them, laid the flashlight on the side of the old sink and grabbed both sides of the cold porcelain basin. In the oval mirror she could see an eerie image—that of a woman with wildly tangled hair, deeply smudged eyes and lips that were vaguely unsteady in the erratic light of the flashlight on the floor.

Shadows played deeply at her cheek and eyes, but nothing could hide the pain cut around her mouth and eyes. She turned on the water, splashed its coldness on her face, then hurried to get dressed again. When she was done, she stood for a long moment in the tiny room, took several lungfuls of air to try to steady herself. Then she took the flashlight and headed back to Ben. She didn't know how to do this, how to lie to him or how to walk away from him.

But she had to. If she didn't love him, it would have been so much easier, but now she had her doubts about even surviving the next few minutes.

BEN WATCHED Reggie walk into the shadows with the dancing light from the flashlight in front of her. Just the sight of her naked made his body stiffen. When she disappeared down the hallway, then a door closed, he sat up. His body was ready to make love to her again, and so was he. But he made himself get up and reach for his jeans. When he slipped them on, he occupied himself with rebuilding the fire, but every sound from deep in the house drew and demanded his attention.

God, he would have never thought he could do this. That he could meet a woman one day and know without a doubt the next day that he wanted her to be with him for the rest of his life. He'd known women before, maybe even loved them a bit, but never enough to want them forever. His hands stilled as he poked at the fire to bring it to new life. Love. It was so simple. He loved her. This was what love was, what it should be. Reggie.

He heard her coming back, and he took his time putting the poker in the holder before he turned. She came into the room right then, dressed again, but her hair was still wildly curling around her face. God, he loved her. But when he would have crossed to her, she lifted one slender hand.

"No, Ben, don't."

She stayed by the door, and despite the roaring fire at his back, a chill started to invade him. Something was very wrong.

"I . . . I need to say something, and—"

He cut off her words by moving to her, despite her objections. He came within inches of her, of lips that tempted him, of breasts rapidly rising and falling under the protection of the crushed white velvet, and he wanted to hold her. But when he would have touched her, she drew back as if he'd burned her.

"No," she gasped.

He pushed his hands behind him, but didn't edge back. "What's going on?"

"Ben, I . . . that is, I have to go."

"No. Don't. Not yet."

She clasped her hands tightly in front of her, and he saw the way she worried her bottom lip with her teeth. Then, with a soft intake of air, she said quickly, "I'm so sorry. So very sorry."

"What—"

"No, just let me say this," she said in a breathless voice. "I don't—I mean, I've never done anything like this before, and I'm so sorry that it happened."

"That we made love?" he asked, his voice tight in his own ears.

Her lashes swept low, shadowing her eyes, and he could see the way she jumped when the logs popped loudly behind them.

"I'm sorry that I was so...so stupid. I had no right to do this."

A tension was growing in him, taking away any lingering pleasure that he'd found with her earlier. "Stupid? You were stupid?"

"I never meant for anything like this to happen." She darted a look at him, then took a step back. "I just have to go now. It's better this way."

"No," he insisted, and she stopped, but wouldn't look back at him. She kept her eyes down, and he needed to look into those amber eyes. This couldn't be happening. It couldn't be true. He closed the distance between them, and despite her instant flinch, he gripped her by the shoulders.

"Look at me, Reggie." When she didn't, he shook her once. "Please, just look at me."

Slowly her lashes raised and he could see a brightness in her eyes, but no tears.

"Ben, please, don't do this."

"Do what? Ask for an explanation? God, after what just happened, don't you at least owe me that much?"

Her tongue flicked out to touch her lips and he could feel his body tighten. It was all he could do not to pull her to him, to taste her and convince her that this was all madness.

"You're right," she whispered.

Her voice was so low that he had to strain to make out her words.

"You deserve that much. Just ... just let me go. Please?"

He reluctantly broke their connection, but didn't move back from her. "Okay, explain."

She took an unsteady breath, then said, "It's wrong. I told you, Dennis, we ... we're ..." She swallowed hard, then went on. "We're going to be married, and for me to do this. It's...it's below contempt. I can't believe that I let things get so out of hand."

"We made love, for God's sake. We both wanted it, didn't we?"

"Yes, no, I ... it doesn't matter. It shouldn't have happened." She took a step back as she spoke. "I can't tell you how sorry I am. I'm just so humiliated, and now I have to figure out what to do to make things right again."

"Stay with me," he said before he knew the words were coming. But that's exactly what he wanted. Reggie. For now. Forever. "Just stay."

She shook her head, and her tangled hair brushed her cheeks. "No, I can't. Dennis, he—"

"Damn Dennis. Let him wait. He's waited this long. He can wait a while longer." He started to go closer, but she immediately moved back again into the foyer. "Okay," he said, holding up both hands palms out toward her. "I shouldn't have said that, but..." He ran a hand roughly over his face, trying to think, trying to find the words to make her stay.

"No, you don't have to apologize. I'm just sorry, so sorry," she said, taking another step back.

"Reggie, stop saying that. Don't do this. At least stay until we get this ironed out." He'd never begged a woman in his life. He'd never begged for anything, even during those years in foster home after foster home. But he'd beg now if he had to. "Please, come back inside and we can talk. I know we can figure this out if you just give it a chance."

He couldn't bear the distance between them, and he took a long stride with his hand out. But Reggie jumped back as if she thought he was going to hurt her. And in the same moment, Mikey let out a scream.

Ben looked over his shoulder, then back at Reggie, and held up a hand palm out to her. "Wait, just wait," he said, then blurted out something that was as true as anything he'd ever uttered in his life. "I love you."

The words rocked his world, but she just stared at him. He heard Mikey cry out again, and he started backward. "Just stay," he said quickly, then hurried to Mikey.

He ran into the smaller room, found Mikey standing in the crib with his hands reaching out. Ben scooped his son up, hugging him to his chest, and carried Mikey back through the living room. As he stepped into the entryway, the lights flashed once, then came on, burning steadily. He blinked at the sudden brilliance, but he didn't need the light to see that the foyer was empty, the door shut tightly. Reggie was gone.

"Oh, man," he breathed.

Then Mikey raised back to look at Ben and touch him on the cheek with one tiny hand. "Daddy, where Geegee?"

Ben stared at the door, his eyes stinging and his heart pounding against his ribs as if he'd run a four-minute mile. He'd had no idea until now that it could hurt like this to love someone completely and blindly.

"Daddeeeeeee," Mikey whined, trying to pull Ben's face around so he had to look at him. "Where Geegee?"

"Reggie's gone," Ben whispered, the words underscoring a horrible, empty feeling inside him.

"Geegee all gone? All gone?"

"Yes, I'm afraid so, Mikey. She's all gone."

"No, all gone. No. No," Mikey said as he hugged Ben around the neck and buried his head in Ben's chest. "No, all gone."

Ben turned from the door. "All gone," he whispered again.

REGGIE WALKED quickly through the night, her eyes on the ground where she stepped, but her mind on the man in the house behind her and his final words. They couldn't be true. They couldn't. They were just a part of this craziness, a justification, maybe. But they couldn't be true.

As she got to the driveway, which was still wet from the storm, she started to run, even though her heels made it more than difficult. As she stepped onto the sidewalk, the streetlights flashed once, then came on in a steady glow. Lights in her house appeared. One look back at the Eatons' place and she could see that the lights were on there, too.

For a split second she thought she saw a shadow in the windows by the door, then it was gone. And she turned from the illusion and ran for her driveway. But as she rounded the hedges, she stopped dead in her tracks.

Dennis's car was parked by the steps, her porch light on and glistening off its wet surface. Her stomach lurched. He had been there all the time, sitting, waiting for her while she'd been with Ben. She almost whirled around and ran. But she knew there was no place to go. No place at all.

She took a breath of the cold, damp air, then slowly approached the car. But it was empty. She looked around, but couldn't see anyone. "Dennis?" she called, then the front door of her house opened and he was there.

"Regina? Is that you?"

"Yes," she said as she started for the porch and up toward Dennis.

He came out toward her, then the next thing she knew, she was being hugged.

"I've been so worried," he said against her hair.

For a moment, she let herself lean against him, needing the support, but she soon pulled back, unable to endure the closeness. "It's cold out here," she said, then moved from him to go into the house.

She stepped inside, into everything familiar and everything the same as when she'd left, except that two candles were burning on the mantel. Yet she felt as different as day from night. She crossed to the fireplace, with its neatly stacked logs that she'd redone that morning, and wished the fire were roaring. Anything to take away this horrible chill deep inside her.

"What happened?" Dennis asked from behind her. "I couldn't get through on the phone, then when the storm eased, I came to get you and you weren't here. The door was open and I'd barely come in, when the storm got worse. I had no idea where you were, and the phone was out, so I couldn't call the restaurant to see if you'd gone down there by mistake."

He touched her shoulder, and she almost jumped out of her skin. Then he turned her slowly, and she could see the way he looked at her.

He drew back and asked, "My God, what happened to you?"

She remembered her image in the mirror in the bathroom and knew there was little in this world that could explain her disheveled appearance. Except one thing, and she couldn't bear to think of that.

As a shiver coursed through her, she moved quickly away from Dennis to cross to the thermostat on the wall by the kitchen door. "What . . . what time is it?" she asked as she fiddled with the setting.

"Almost midnight. Regina, you look as if . . ." His words trailed off, as though he was at a loss even to think of what could have happened to her.

She closed her eyes tightly, then turned and opened them, to find Dennis still by the hearth. She looked down at her mussed dress, and the memory of Ben taking it off her came with stunning clarity. She hugged herself, damning the cold that wouldn't leave, angry with herself for everything.

"I was out and the storm came and I . . . I took refuge at a neighbor's house. He . . . they let me stay until it stopped raining, then I walked back here." The lie came easily to her, and why not. She'd told the biggest lie of all to Ben. A small lie was easy. "The storm was just . . . terrible." She shivered again and could barely contain it. "Now my dress is ruined."

Dennis crossed to her, but didn't touch her. "You look half-frozen. What you need is a good hot bath, then a sound sleep."

He touched her cheek with fingers so cold that they made her tremble again.

"You could have caught a chill going out like that. Where did you go anyway?"

"Just to take a neighbor something." She hugged herself more tightly. "I think you're right. I need a hot bath."

He smiled slightly at her. "Our evening out just isn't happening, is it? But that's okay. We'll do it again, and the next time, believe me, everything will go perfectly. I promise we'll have our talk." He leaned toward her and brushed a feather-light kiss on her lips before drawing back. "Now, have a good night, and I'll call you in the morning."

She nodded, then he turned and headed for the door. He opened the door, letting in more cold, then looked across at her. "Fate can't keep doing this to us, can it?"

"No...it can't," she whispered as another shiver hit her.

"Do you want me to stay to help?" he asked.

She shook her head. "A hot bath. Sleep. I'll be fine." Another lie.

He touched his fingertips to her lips, then with a nod left, closing the door behind him. As she heard his car start, she slowly sank down until she was sitting on the floor against the wall. She wrapped her arms around her legs and rested her forehead on her knees as the shivering grew. "I'll be fine," she murmured through clenched teeth to the emptiness that surrounded her.

ANGELINA HOVERED near Reggie, thankful that Miss Victoria wouldn't have any reason to be checking on the situation at least for a while. She'd seen sudden breakups before, goodness knows, but Reggie and Ben just outdid all the others. Even the prince and princess had given some warning of their intentions. That monumental failure had been laid on someone else. But this was all hers.

"Ah, Reggie," she whispered as she watched the poor woman sitting on the floor alone. "I think I understand what you're doing, but I can't let you do it. At least, not without a fight."

She saw Reggie push herself to her feet, then move to the fireplace and stare into the hearth.

If humans had any sense at all, they'd make this business so much easier. Angelina sat on the hearth, looking up at Reggie. "You love him. I know you do. And he loves you. But you're being so noble. You're giving him up so he can find someone who will make him happy. Foolish, foolish human. You can't see the answers even when they're right there in front of you."

Angelina stood and crossed her arms. "You're forcing me to pull out all the stops if you don't go back and see Ben again."

When Reggie sighed, then turned and moved across the room, Angelina almost thought she'd managed to get the idea through to Reggie. But disappointment was hers when Reggie walked right past the front door, then the phone, and back toward her bedroom. Angelina saw her go into the room, walk right through it to the bathroom, then start steaming water into the old claw-foot tub. As Reggie stripped off her clothes, Angelina backed out of the room, then waved herself back to headquarters.

Pull out all the stops, she thought as she glided into her seat, sat back and looked at the file on Reggie and Ben. She took out both pictures, laid them side by side on her glass desk, then found a smaller photo of Mikey. She laid the child's photo between the two adults' pictures, and smiled.

"That's it. A child will lead them." She tapped Mikey's photo. "Yes, I think that will work nicely.

Chapter Thirteen

Reggie didn't know why she went home. But as she walked into the house she'd been brought up in, she felt a sense of familiarity that seemed almost welcome after the turmoil of the past few days. And that was a definite first—finding any form of peace at this house.

She stood in the living room of the sprawling ranch house, listened, and for a moment thought she was in some sort of twilight zone. There wasn't a sound anywhere, just the fragrance of a turkey roast, and maybe the aroma of coffee mixing with that scent.

"Hello?" she called out, her voice echoing in the rooms done in a style she'd always called "early garage sale"—pieces mixed and matched over the years, used by nine children and in someway fitting together.

"Regina, is that you?"

She heard her mother's voice and headed toward it as she unbuttoned the jacket she was wearing over jeans and a blouse. "Yes, it's me," she said as she stepped into the huge kitchen.

Her mother was by the stove, stirring something that was releasing steam into the air of the yellow-and-white space. "Well, this is a nice surprise," her mother said as she turned and smiled at her. "I was wondering if you even got my messages."

Annie Clark was a tiny woman, hardly the kind you'd think would have nine children in nineteen years. She was a smaller version of Melanie, and right now, in a pair of jeans and loose shirt, she looked as if she could be a teenager. Until you saw the streaks of gray in her short dark hair and the lines at her eyes and mouth.

"Melanie said she was going over to see you and find out what was going on," her mother said as she laid a spoon on a plate on the counter, then turned and wiped her hands together.

Reggie crossed to the table in the breakfast area of the kitchen and dropped onto one of the mismatched wooden chairs by the huge round table. "Mel? No, I haven't seen her." She glanced at the double ovens. "Turkey?"

"Two of them."

She almost asked why, but realized today was Thanksgiving. "They smell good."

Her mother crossed to the table, then sank into a chair opposite Reggie. "So, if Melanie didn't go to see you...." She sat forward, clasping her hands on the table in front of her. "So, tell me what's going on with you? We hardly get to talk anymore."

"We've never had much time to talk," she said before she could catch the words back.

Her mother frowned. "We haven't? I thought we talked a lot." She shrugged. "Take off your jacket and I can make us some hot chocolate."

"No, thanks," Reggie said, keeping her jacket on. For the past few days nothing had settled well for her, least of all the knowledge that Ben was moving in next door. And all the hot chocolate in the world wouldn't help that. "Where is everyone?"

"At church. Dad took them so I could get everything done in time for the dinner tonight." She exhaled. "So, Melanie tells me you're getting new neighbors. I always liked the Eatons. Nice people. I'm sorry they're moving, but from what I hear they're going to be near their grandchildren. So, who's moving in?"

Reggie stood and crossed to the coffeepot. Maybe something hot would help after all. As she poured herself a cup, she said, "A pediatrician."

"Any children?" her mother asked behind her.

"Just one," she said, then took a breath before she turned and went back to the table to sit down. She cradled the mug between her hands and knew she wasn't going to be able to live there anymore. There was no peace in that house, not knowing Ben would be so close. She could find another place, where she could walk out the door and not worry about seeing him.

She didn't want a repeat of less than a hour ago— her looking out her kitchen window and seeing Ben over at the house, Mikey in his arms. No, she didn't want that to happen again.

"So?" her mother said.

"Excuse me?"

"I was wondering what's going on."

"I just dropped by for a minute," she murmured.

"Regina, I can count on one hand the number of times you've just dropped by. Does this have anything to do with the other night when we had that horrible storm?"

Reggie sighed. The woman could hit the nail on the head without even knowing there was a nail to hit. "Why do you ask that?"

"Well, Dennis called and said you weren't at the house when he went to pick you up. He sounded quite concerned. Then he called back later and told your dad that you were just fine."

"He had no reason to be concerned," she said.

"He's quite important to you, isn't he?"

Reggie sipped her coffee and wished she hadn't. Her stomach was rebelling big-time, and she sat back, pressing a hand to her middle. "He's a friend."

"Melanie hinted he might be more than that," Mrs. Clark said in an oddly flat voice.

Reggie fingered her empty mug. It had been a blessing not to have to see Dennis just yet. But she knew that in a few hours, she'd have to face him and tell the truth. "What would you think if he was?"

"Your life is your life, Regina, and all I want is for you to be happy." Mrs. Clark sat back and asked, "So, are you?"

Reggie wasn't up to any of this, and wished she hadn't come. But when she knew she should just stand and leave, she found herself asking her mother something she never thought she would. "Do you and Dad love each other?"

Her mother didn't look shocked by the question at all. She just said, "Why are you asking?"

"I was just wondering. With nine kids, how could you ever have time to be together?"

"You mean in the biblical sense?" Her mother laughed at her own joke.

Reggie stood and carried her mug to the sink, decidedly sorry she'd asked at all. "I have to go."

"Regina," her mother said. "I love your father more than anyone in this world. Does that answer your question?"

She put the mug down, then turned without going back to the window. "I guess so."

Her mother stood and crossed to where she stood. "Oh, I get it. You want to know if it's the sort of love where the world moves and rockets go off?"

She'd never seen this side of her mother before. A woman, a woman in love. "That's silly," she declared.

"No, it's not. When I first met your father I couldn't breathe when I was near him. When he walked into a room, the world was right. And it's still that way. I might be fifty years old, but your dad is still the center of everything for me."

"But you had nine children."

"We certainly did. By choice. Oh, not the number. But we both wanted a large family. I know that's not the choice of many anymore, but we wanted it. And I've never regretted that for a minute." She crossed her arms on her chest and eyed Reggie. "I know you never understood that, but I couldn't explain it, either. This is what I wanted, Reggie."

"But you and Dad hardly had time for each other."

That brought a smile from her mother. "Oh, we had time. We made time. When two people are in love, things don't have to be one long honeymoon. Just being near that person is enough sometimes." The smile faded to a concerned frown. "You're thinking of marrying Dennis Benning, aren't you?"

"He hasn't asked me."

"But he will. I could tell when you brought him over here that he was going to...sooner or later. Just one question?"

"What?"

"Do you love him?"

Reggie closed her eyes, but opened them immediately when images sprang to life in her of Ben making love to her. She couldn't think of love without Ben being right in the middle of it. "No, I don't," she muttered.

"Good."

"You don't like him?"

"Oh, I think he's just fine...for someone. But not you."

A door opened and Reggie heard her father call out, "Annie, we're back."

Then the others were coming into the room. Everyone was there, talking at the same time, looking into the oven, sniffing the turkey scent in the air. Her father hugged her, dropped a kiss on her forehead, then crossed to follow the others opening the oven to look at the turkeys.

"Smells great, Annie," he said.

Reggie knew she had to go. But when she would have, her mother touched her arm. "You'll be back for dinner, won't you?"

There was no way she wanted to have dinner with her brothers and sisters and parents. Not today. But she knew she'd be back more often than she had been before. "I'm sorry. Dennis is coming over later, and mentioned something about dinner. So I don't think so."

"I'd tell you to bring him home, since there's always room for one more, but the man would probably have an apoplectic fit if he sat down to Thanksgiving dinner with all of us."

Reggie could actually smile at that. "You're right. Now I have to go." With a quick hug for her mother, and after saying goodbyes to everyone, she went back through the house and out into the chilly November air.

She pulled her jacket more tightly around her and headed for her car, bracing herself for what she knew she had to do to settle her life again.

BEN CLOSED the door after the movers finished with their work, then went upstairs with Mikey and gave him to the nanny. "I'll be downstairs working on the boxes in the living room. When you get Mikey to sleep, try to make some sense out of the bedrooms," he said. She nodded, then took Mikey into his room, the one that looked out over the huge oak where Ben was going to build a tree house. For Mikey, and for himself just a bit.

He went down into the living room and started on the boxes he'd packed. His furniture seemed skimpy in the large rooms of the house, and he knew he'd have to get more soon. And he'd have to buy some carpets for the floors. His gaze went to the fireplace and the bare spot in front of the hearth. Yes, definitely rugs.

He went to the small desk he'd had the movers put by the front windows and undid the top box sitting in a pile by it. Inside were the papers from the agency, which he needed to fill in to start the adoption process for another child. He took them out, then reached for a nearby chair and sat down. He scanned the papers, then dropped them onto the desk.

All he'd thought about for so long was his family. All he'd thought he wanted was kids and more kids. Kids to fill his life and make it whole. But right then he knew that kids weren't for fixing lives. Oh, he'd been so happy with Mikey. He couldn't love him more if he was his biological child. And Mikey had filled a vast emptiness in his life.

But now he knew that a new emptiness had been torn in him. An emptiness that had come when Reggie had walked out. For a few brief moments in time he'd been complete, then the pain had begun. He turned from the papers and crossed to the hearth. With quick, angry movements he built a fire, then struck the kindling and watched the wood flame.

A family—that's what he'd always wanted, what he'd always wished for. But damn it all, he wanted that family to include Reggie. Just Reggie and Mikey. He sank onto the hearth as he realized that he'd finally figured out what a family really was. It wasn't numbers. It was loving, and he loved Reggie. Simple. Painfully simple.

He picked up a loose piece of kindling that had fallen on the hearth and tossed it into the fire. Reggie. She was just next door, but a thousand miles couldn't have been a bigger gulf between them. She was sorry they'd made love, and she was embarrassed. Her words haunted him day and night. And he was tired of sitting there not doing anything.

He stood and crossed to the front windows to look out at the high hedges between their properties. Through a gap he could see the back of her house, a window that was probably the kitchen. She was in there. She was so close, and he had to figure out some way to bridge the gap between them.

DENNIS HAD TOLD Reggie he would be by to pick her up at six, and with one minute to go before six o'clock, the doorbell rang. Reggie stood alone in the kitchen, bracing herself. She wasn't anxious to do this, but she had to. Dennis deserved better than her, and she knew now that she'd never loved him. She never could. So she couldn't marry him. It wasn't going to be easy, but when he left tonight, he wouldn't be coming back.

When the bell rang a second time, she called out, "I'll be right there." Then, dressed in a white silk blouse and simple navy slacks, she went through the house to respond.

When she opened the door, she was shocked to see not only Dennis, but a man and woman on either side of him. And she didn't have to be introduced to know that the two people had to be his parents. His father was an older version of Dennis—a bit more weight, a bit less hair, but the same way of standing, and wearing the same type of three-piece suit.

The woman was tiny and elegant, with diamonds at her throat, a mink stole over her shoulders and gray-blue hair cut very short and immaculately styled. Her simple gray suit must have cost a fortune.

"Regina, I hope you don't mind, but after trying several times to be alone with you to ask you if you would meet with my parents, I decided that I should just do it. They agreed that it might be a very nice thing to have Thanksgiving dinner together at the Scullery in town."

She was almost speechless. His parents. He hadn't been about to ask her to marry him. Then she understood—he'd wanted her to pass muster first. All she'd wanted to do was to break off with Dennis, not meet his mother and father. She realized she was staring and Dennis was saying something she wasn't catching. "I...excuse me. Come in, please."

She stood back to let them in, then closed the door and turned. Dennis was helping his mother take off her stole, and his father was taking off his overcoat and laying it precisely across the back of the high-backed chair. Just the way Dennis had done several times.

Dennis turned to Reggie with the fur piece. "Where shall I put this?" he asked.

She crossed to him and stammered, "I'll take care of it." She was close enough to whisper to Dennis, "You should have told me your parents were coming."

He smiled at her. "I thought that since I'd met your family, it was high time you met mine." He leaned toward her and touched her cheek with his cool lips. "I wanted very much for them to get to know you."

She held the fur in her hands, dumbfounded by this twist of fate. A problem that she didn't want at all. "While I put this away, why don't you get out some wine? I think there's a bottle of something red in the cupboard over the refrigerator and the glasses are with it."

"Of course."

He went past her, back to where his parents were, but Reggie didn't look back as she took the fur piece into the bedroom. She dropped it on the bed, a bit nauseated by the feel of fur that had once been a living animal.

Leaving it on the bed, she went back into the living room, to find Mr. and Mrs. Benning sitting side by side on the couch. The father was leaning back, staring at the fireplace, and the mother sat gingerly on the edge of the cushions. As Reggie sat down in a chair by the hearth, she had the thought that Mrs. Benning looked like a very rich bird.

"I'm sorry. Dennis didn't even tell me he was bringing the two of you, and I'm totally unprepared."

Dennis came back into the room carrying the bottle of wine and four glasses. "Regina, don't fuss so. This is not a formal thing. I just wanted us all to talk for a bit. Then we have reservations for dinner at seven-thirty."

He put the glasses on the side table, poured the wine into them, then handed one to each of his parents, then one to Reggie. He raised his glass. "Happy Thanksgiving."

His parents silently lifted their glasses, and so did Reggie. She drank her wine in one long gulp, then cradled the crystal goblet between her hands.

"So, Miss Clark, our Dennis tells us that you met him at a . . . a bookstore?" Mrs. Benning said.

"Yes, it's where I work, and please, call me 'Reggie.'" When the woman frowned, she added quickly, "Or 'Regina.'"

The woman nodded regally. "Our Dennis tells us that you are one of nine children."

"Yes."

"My, I had no idea that people still had large families." She glanced toward the silent Mr. Benning. "Dennis senior and I decided right away that we would have one child and give our offspring everything we could. I believe that with more than one child, there just is not enough quality time or attention to go around. One has to question the wisdom of having multiple children. Doesn't one?"

Reggie had spent her life hearing remarks about her family, about rabbits breeding, and she'd taken them in her stride. Probably because she'd basically believed the same things herself. But Mrs. Benning was hitting a nerve, one that Reggie hadn't even known was there before.

"I believe people should have as many or as few children as they want and can provide for," Reggie said.

Mrs. Benning raised one finely penciled eyebrow. "You believe that having nine children is a rational thing to do?"

"I don't know," Reggie admitted.

"You perhaps wish to have a large family?"

"Oh, no," Dennis said quickly. "Regina and I have discussed this, and we're one in the belief that children do not make a marriage."

Reggie could almost see Mrs. Benning's relief at her son's words.

"Ah, so true." She looked at Reggie. "How sensible of you, dear. And believe me, Dennis has mentioned his great affection for you. But I want to assure you on one point. We do not require the egocentric procreation of ourselves in the form of a great many grandchildren. One would be just fine. A boy, like our Dennis."

Reggie stared at her, only inbred good manners keeping her from saying that she hoped the two of them would never see grandchildren. Little copies of them running around in the world. She must be close to hysteria, she decided, when laughter almost bubbled up in her. "Well, that's a good thing to know," she murmured.

"I told my mother and father about the disaster in your garden room."

"Yes, indeed he did." Mrs. Benning took a sip of the wine, vaguely wrinkled her nose, then added, "I do not see why people have children when they can't possibly control them. Dennis was such a sweet child, so orderly and obedient. He was never any trouble."

Reggie could believe that completely. "He sounds like a perfect son, Mrs. Benning."

"Perfect indeed," she said with a small smile—the first warmth Reggie had seen in the woman. "Wasn't he?" she asked her husband.

He nodded. "Quite right, my dear," Mr. Benning said in a scratchy voice.

"I would warrant he was very unlike that little hooligan who destroyed your plants."

Reggie didn't know where it came from, but the mention of Mikey in that tone snapped something in her. "Mikey, the child in question, was terrified. He accidentally got locked in the room and couldn't get out. He's had a very sad background."

"No doubt, with a father who can't control him," she sniffed disdainfully.

"He was adopted just a few months ago."

"Oh, well, that likely accounts for it. One never knows what one is getting in an adoption."

That drove Reggie to her feet and in a split second she knew that manners weren't important anymore. "Mrs. Benning," she said. "Mikey is the dearest little boy in the world, and his father is the best father I have ever seen. He loves Mikey and they're very fortunate to have found each other."

"Well, of course, I wasn't saying they weren't." She waved one hand imperially. "I was just stating a fact about the chance one takes—"

"Mrs. Benning, this discussion is over." Reggie put her glass down and was ready to ask them all to leave. Especially Dennis, who was sitting there smiling at his mother, as if what she was saying was just fine by him. Smug, contemptible man.

But a banging on the back door stopped her. It sounded as if something was being hit against the door, over and over again.

"Oh, my dear, what in the world?" Mrs. Benning asked.

Without saying a thing, Reggie hurried past the Bennings toward the noise. By the time she got to the back door on the garden room, she heard more than the banging. She heard a little voice saying, "Geegee! Geegee! Where you? Where you?"

Reggie opened the door and Mikey was there, dressed in red blanket pajamas. "Mikey, what are you doing here?" she asked as she reached to pick him up. She glanced around the backyard to the hedges, but couldn't see Ben anywhere. "Where's Daddy?"

"Gone, all gone," he said as he flung his little arms out to his sides and held his hands palms up. "Daddy allllll gone."

Reggie almost went out to go to Ben's house right then, but something stopped her. She looked at Mikey and smiled. "Want to meet some new people?"

"Huh," he said with a grin and a shake of his head that made his blond hair ruffle.

"Okay, boy, let's do it," she murmured, and went back inside, closing the door behind them. She walked into the living room, and Dennis stood as soon as she entered the room.

"Regina, what's going on?" he asked as she came over to the hearth with Mikey in her arms to face the silent Bennings.

"He came to visit, so I thought I'd bring him in and let him meet all of you."

She looked at Mr. and Mrs. Benning, who were staring at her as if she were holding the plague in her arms. "Mikey, this is Mr. and Mrs. Benning. Say hi to them."

Mikey held more tightly to her neck, but managed a small "Hi."

Mrs. Benning stared at the child. "What is this?"

"Who, Mrs. Benning. Who. His name is Michael Grant. He lives next door. The hooligan? You remember. He's adopted, and he smashed all my plants in the garden room."

"I hardly think this is amusing, Regina," Mrs. Benning sniffed.

"You're right. It's not." Mikey buried his face in her neck and hugged her harder. And something in Reggie just slipped into place, quietly, but ever so neatly. She could love this child the way she loved his father. And that thought stopped her dead. She knew she loved Ben, but this child? She shifted him more tightly to her chest. "And I am not amused by any of this."

Mr. Benning finally moved. He stood up, then looked at Dennis. "I believe we need to get going to make those reservations, son."

Dennis had been sitting there just staring, saying nothing, but now he spoke. "Regina, give the boy back to your neighbor and get ready for dinner."

She gazed at Dennis and the words came with none of the trauma she had dreaded would come with them. "I'm not going." She shifted Mikey a bit higher in her arms. "I need to take care of Mikey. You go ahead and have a lovely meal."

Mrs. Benning also stood. "My dear, we planned for this evening, and if your neighbor can't keep his child in sight, I don't see what that has to do with us. Plans *are* plans, however."

"Yes, you're very right. You don't see what it has to do with us. But I do." She looked at Dennis. "I'm sorry," she said softly. "I'm not going."

He didn't move for a moment, then very slowly he came toward her. "Regina?"

"It's no use. I can't do it anymore."

He stood very still, then nodded, his mouth tight. "Are you sure?"

"Very sure," she affirmed, although she hated to do this to him.

He turned from her, then spoke to his parents. "It seems our plans have changed. Regina won't be accompanying us to dinner after all."

"Well," his mother sniffed. And his father said nothing.

Reggie carried Mikey into the bedroom, retrieved the fur piece, then went back out to hand it to Dennis. "Your mother's stole."

He took it from her, then helped his mother put it on. At the front door, as he opened it for his parents, Dennis stopped and looked back at Reggie. "You won't change your mind?"

"No, I won't," she said. "But thanks."

Mrs. Benning nodded to Reggie. "Good evening. You shall be missed, Regina." Then she took her husband's arm and walked out the door. Dennis glanced back, then followed them.

As the door closed, she muttered, "But you won't be." She buried her face in Mikey's hair for a long moment, then as the little boy started to squirm, she drew back and looked down into his big brown eyes. "You're quite a kid, Mikey," she whispered. "I've never seen a house clear so quickly as this one just did. You did good."

He grinned at her. "Huh," he said with a quick nod, then, "Daddy?"

"Yeah, let's go find your daddy and let him know you're okay." As she went back through the house to the garden room, she faltered. Seeing Ben again wasn't what she wanted to do right now, but she had no choice. *Just do it and get it over with,* she told herself. *Just do it.*

She stepped out into the garden room, then stopped in her tracks. Ben was there, just standing by the open back door, watching her and Mikey. "You," she breathed. Mikey turned, then squirmed to be let down. But even as she released him, she didn't look away from Ben.

"Yes, it's me," he said. "I was just coming to see if Mikey was here."

Mikey ran to his father and Ben picked him up without looking away from Reggie.

"He...just showed up at the back door. I was coming to take him home."

"I would have gone to the front door," Ben said as he put Mikey down again, "but I saw that big

Mercedes out in front and thought your fiancé was probably over. I didn't want to intrude."

"You didn't. They've left." She held herself more tightly, each tiny thing about Ben burning in her mind. Did a woman ever forget about loving someone, about the way he touched her, the way he held her? She shook her head to try to stop the thoughts that bombarded her. "And Mikey's fine."

"I can see he is," Ben said as he glanced at the boy, who was scrambling up on one of the chairs to the wrought-iron table set by the screened-in windows where Reggie had kept her plants. "He's so quick I can hardly keep up with him."

"He's quick, okay," she said.

"We can't do it, can we?"

"I'm sorry?"

"Talk about this."

"Mikey's fine. He didn't do any damage this time," she said.

"I wasn't talking about Mikey. I meant about the night of the storm. We aren't going to be able to talk about it, are we?"

"No." She could feel her expression tightening. "We can't."

"I asked you to wait."

"I had to go."

"Reggie, I . . ." He exhaled again, then tucked his fingertips in the pockets of his jeans and hunched his shoulders slightly. "Just tell me one thing."

Chapter Fourteen

Reggie stayed very still. "If I can," she said softly.

"Why did it happen?"

Because I love you, she wanted to say, but knew she couldn't. "I don't know," she lied, and hated herself for it. "But it did, and we just have to forget it."

His eyes narrowed, as if he couldn't bear looking at her. "And if I can't? What then?"

She shrugged, her insides so knotted that she could barely breathe. "Ben, don't do this." She took a step back. "I think you'd better leave."

"What if I told you I can't forget about it? That every time I look over here, I hope I see you."

She bit her lip hard. "You...you won't have to worry about that much longer. I'm going to—"

"I know," he said. "You're really going to marry this Dennis person and move into his place."

She started to tell him that wasn't it at all, that she was going to sell her house just so she couldn't walk out her door and see him. But she never got to say that. As she started to turn away, to say the words while she was getting away from Ben, she saw Mikey.

He had one foot on the chair, his other knee on the tabletop, and he was trying to pull himself up onto the table. But it didn't work.

She saw the table wobble, and the world shifted to slow motion. The chair was slipping backward to the tiles, and Mikey was pitching off to one side. She saw him falling headfirst toward the tiles, his arms outspread, and Ben lunging toward him at the same time she did. The screams—hers, Ben's and Mikey's—mingled in a horrible cacophony that only broke when Mikey hit the tiles.

Suddenly everything sped up to a frightening speed—Ben grabbing Mikey, almost knocking her sideways, then blood everywhere, blond hair stained, the tiles stained and Mikey screaming even louder. Reggie looked in horror at the toddler, his face covered with blood, and his cries tore at her.

"Get a towel, anything clean to stop the bleeding," Ben snapped as he turned Mikey to face him.

Reggie ran into the kitchen and grabbed a clean white rag. She got back outside to find Ben with his hand on Mikey's wound and blood oozing from between his fingers. He took the folded towel, then pressed it to Mikey's head and the boy screamed even more.

"Oh, God, is he okay?" Reggie asked.

"I've got to get him to the ER." He shifted the child to one shoulder, smearing blood across his shirt in the process, then looked at Reggie. "Where's your car?"

"In the garage. I can get it out."

"Never mind. Mine's right out in front of my house." He turned and ran for the door, throwing it open so sharply that it cracked back against the screen frame.

Then Reggie was going after him. She barely kept up with his long stride as he ran for the Jeep, then they were at his car and she gasped, "Give me Mikey. You drive."

He turned to her as if he was shocked she was still with him, then simply handed her the little boy. Mikey had stopped crying, and that almost scared Reggie as much as his crying had. She knew about kids and head injuries, about keeping them awake, but when she looked at Mikey, his eyes were partly open, and his skin was horribly pale.

She gathered him to her and cuddled him in her arms, uncaring that the bloody shirt was between his head and her blouse. Ben opened the car door for her, then helped her get in with Mikey. He slammed the door shut, sprinted around and got behind the wheel. He started the car, and the tires squealed on the driveway as he drove off toward the street.

He glanced at Reggie and said, "If you notice anything different about him, let me know."

"Different?"

"Labored breathing, muscle twitches, shaking. Anything. Okay?"

"Yes, yes, okay."

As he drove onto the street and took off south, Ben reached for his cell phone, which was lying on the console. He flipped it open, hit a couple of numbers, then spoke quickly. "Dr. Grant. Have ER ready for a head wound, male, two years, O positive. Tell Kelly to meet me at the doors if he's there. Good." He flipped the phone shut, then looked at Reggie again. "How is he?"

"Okay, but he's so still."

Ben touched Mikey on the leg. "You're going to be okay, champ. Daddy's going to make very sure of that."

Mikey took a shuddering breath, and Reggie could feel his little heart hammering against her. "Sure, you'll be fine," she murmured. "You're lucky you've got a daddy who's a doctor. He can make everything better."

She met Ben's gaze for a moment, and she wasn't prepared for a flash of what she would have called pain in the blue depths.

"I wish that were true," he whispered, then turned from her and concentrated on his driving.

And in that moment she knew she'd do anything necessary to take the pain away from Ben and Mikey.

The five minutes needed to get to the hospital seemed like an eternity to Reggie. But when the car screeched to a halt by the ER doors, everything happened fast. Ben was out of the car, running around to her side, then two orderlies were coming toward the Jeep with a stretcher, and a doctor came running out after them. He spoke quickly to Ben, then looked at Reggie.

"We'll take it from here."

For some reason she couldn't begin to fathom, she didn't want to hand Mikey off to strangers. He was so small, and so frightened. "I'll carry him inside," she said, and didn't wait for their agreement. She just turned and headed for the doors.

Ben was there, opening the doors for her, then he touched her arm. "This way," he said.

She carried Mikey into the waiting room, then Ben led the way through double metal doors and into a cubicle to the right.

"Let's take a look at the damage," the other doctor said as he came in after them.

"Put him on the examination table, Reggie," Ben said from beside her.

She moved to the table, but when she would have laid Mikey down, he clung to her more tightly and whimpered, "No, no."

She looked at Ben. "Can't I hold him while the doctor examines the wound?"

Ben looked from her to Mikey, then said softly, "Sure. If it helps him. Thanks for doing this."

She wanted to say she couldn't have done anything else, but didn't get a chance to when the doctor came around.

"I'll have to look at the wound," he said. "Sit down there, and lay him back in your arms."

Reggie backed up and sat on the hard chair by the table, then lowered Mikey carefully until he was cradled in her arms. His huge brown eyes stared up at her, and she knew that she'd do anything for this child. When the doctor began to ease the towel from the wound, the little boy's lips began to quiver.

She spoke softly to him. "It's okay, Mikey. This man's a doctor just like Daddy, and he's going to make your boo-boo better." She looked up at Ben. "Where's his bow?"

Ben felt in his pocket, then pulled out the pacifier and gave it to Mikey.

"Mommy knows just what you need, doesn't she, little guy?" the doctor asked as he got the shirt completely clear of the bloody wound. "That's what mommies are for."

She started to tell the doctor she wasn't Mikey's mother, but kept silent when she met Ben's gaze over the doctor's head. He didn't offer to correct the doctor's assumption, either. He just looked at Reggie intently, then down at Mikey again.

A nurse brought in cotton, which the doctor laid on the gash. "It's clean," he told Ben. "Straight. Must have hit on a sharp edge. I'll call Heron down to do the closing. He's upstairs now. Then we'll keep Mikey for a few hours just for observation."

"Thanks, Kelly, I appreciate it," Ben said as he raked his fingers through his hair.

"No problem. We'll take him in now and get him prepped, and when Heron gets here, he'll be ready." The doctor turned to the nurse by the door. "Get a gurney for the child, Nurse."

She hurried out and the doctor looked from Ben to Reggie. "As for you two, go get some coffee and clean up. I'll have you paged when we're done. It'll probably take an hour with everything."

"But we can't just leave Mikey," Reggie said.

"You can't be in there when we work on him," the doctor said. "Ben wouldn't let a parent of his patient be in there, would you, Ben?"

Ben exhaled. "He's right, Reggie. It's just easier this way. Get it over with, then I'll be there when Mikey's done."

She wanted to tell them it was stupid to throw the child in with strangers, but she realized that she had no say in what happened here. She had no place here at all. "All right, I..." She looked down at Mikey, and was shocked to see he was asleep. "Ben, he's sleeping."

"It's okay. They'll monitor him, and he's tired," he said. "All that crying. He's okay. Trust me."

The nurse was there, easing Mikey away from her, and when the woman stood back with the sleeping toddler in her arms, Reggie felt a sense of loss that was staggering. She quickly covered her feelings by standing and brushing at her slacks and blouse. She averted her eyes from the bloody mess on the silk, and found herself feeling vaguely faint.

She watched as the nurse carried Mikey to the gurney, then laid him on it, and the little boy didn't waken. Reggie closed her eyes when they wheeled him out of sight, and when she opened them, Ben was there, right in front of her. She saw the blood staining his shirt, and before she knew what she was doing, she raised a hand to touch a spot by his heart. "He bled so much," she breathed. "And he's so little."

"He'll be fine. Kelly and Heron are the best."

He touched her chin, cupping it with his warmth, and she felt her head start to get lighter.

"I don't know how to thank you for all that you did," he told her.

"I... I'm sorry for what happened," she said.

"It's my fault. I'm the one who took Mikey over to your house in the first place."

"What?"

"I wanted to talk to you, and I couldn't think of how else to do it."

That only confused her more. "I'm sorry it turned out this way."

"You're always saying you're sorry to me."

He smiled—a crooked expression that touched her.

"Please, don't do that again."

Without warning, he leaned down and brushed his lips against hers. As he drew back, the room began to spin and the world started to recede precariously. She heard herself saying, "Oh, I'm sorry..." Then she fell forward into Ben.

In the next instant, she was in his arms, being gathered to his chest and held the way she remembered from before. For a moment she let herself lean on Ben, let herself feel his heart beat against her cheek and let his warmth invade her being. It felt so good, so right, and that's when she pushed to move back. She couldn't afford to let herself get used to any of this, no matter how enticing it was to her.

Ben let her go, then studied her face for a moment. "Come on. We can't go in with Mikey, and I've got connections here." He slipped his arm around her shoulder with a familiarity that seemed so natural, then led her to an inside door. "I think I can scare up someplace quiet to wait, and a couple of clean T-shirts." He glanced back and said to a nurse behind them, "We'll be in 750. Call me as soon as Mikey's finished and I can see him."

"Yes, Dr. Grant," the nurse replied.

Reggie moved away from Ben as they walked out into the corridor, but went with him to the elevators.

Neither spoke on the way up to the seventh floor, and by the time they stepped into an empty room at the end of the main corridor, Reggie knew she should have just walked out and left downstairs.

She crossed the green-tiled room to the windows and looked out at the night filled with stars and the beginning of a rising moon. "He'll be okay, won't he?" she asked.

"He's tough," Ben said from somewhere behind her. Then a low light snapped on and she turned at the same moment Ben shrugged out of his blood-stained shirt. The moment echoed the one on the stormy night when his shirt had been soaked from the rain. And her reaction was every bit as strong as it had been then.

As he tossed the shirt on the floor by a side chair, he said, "I'll get the clean shirts," and crossed to a cabinet on the wall by the open door to a bathroom.

Reggie watched him take something out of the cabinet, then he turned with two folded T-shirts in his hands.

"I can't tell you how much it meant to have you here. For Mikey, and for me," he murmured.

"I can't believe that happened. The poor little thing." She trembled at the memory of Mikey diving for the floor. "He was so good, wasn't he?"

Ben studied her, his eyes narrowed, then he threw the shirts onto the bed. "Kelly thought you were his mother."

She looked away from Ben, anywhere but at that expression in his eyes. "I know. I should have said something, but..." She touched her tongue to her lips.

"I thought he'd know you weren't married since you work here."

"Kelly's new. Just came to us from San Francisco. He just assumed—"

"Ah, another person who assumes things," she murmured, shocked that she could actually make a stab at humor, especially now.

His smile came, an endearing one that made her heart lurch.

"You're contagious, aren't you?" he asked.

"I guess so." The humor was quickly gone when Ben cupped her chin lightly with one hand.

"Reggie, I know you're getting married, and I know that Dennis is your fiancé, but I have to say something. I couldn't live with myself if I didn't."

"Ben, Dennis and I..."

He shushed her softly. "No, just listen to me. Then I won't say anything else. Please?"

She moved back from his caress, and he made himself draw his hand back. The woman touched his heart so deeply that he couldn't begin to comprehend it. To have her here with Mikey, holding his son, had been like a lifeline to him. Reggie. His lifeline. And he knew as he looked at her that was just what she was. Or maybe more accurately, his heart line. Everything about her went straight to his heart. And he couldn't let her walk out again. He wouldn't.

"Do you want to sit down or change first?"

She cast him a lash-shadowed glance from amber eyes, then said quietly, "No."

He took a breath, and now that he had her alone, had all of her attention, he didn't know where to begin. If he could touch her again, he knew he'd be centered, but he couldn't do that. If she walked out, he knew that he couldn't bear the lingering memory of touching her again.

He exhaled, then just started talking. "When I saw you with Mikey downstairs I realized something very important."

She just kept looking at him, not talking, and he rushed on. "I've always wanted a family. I've always wanted kids. And I've always wanted to have a home." He exhaled again, then said, "And I've always been wrong."

She frowned slightly, drawing a fine line between her amber eyes. "Wrong?"

"What I've been looking for, and didn't know it, was love. Pure and simple. Love. Loving someone, someone loving me. And I found it with Mikey. He's as much my son as any biological child could be. He's everything I've been looking for rolled up in one little boy." He hesitated, then knew he had to say it. If she threw it back at him, at least he would have said it. "Then a miracle happened. Poof. Magic. I found it again. With you."

When she didn't move or say anything, he went on quickly, "Reggie, I know you've got Dennis and you're going to marry him, but could you hold off on it, just for a bit? Just give me a chance?" He turned from her, unable to bear her wide-eyed gaze any longer. He raked his fingers through his hair and closed his eyes so tightly that colors exploded behind his lids. "God help me, I love you, Reggie. I've never loved a woman the way I love you, and I'm too late.

You found Dennis, then I found you, and I'm not sure what to do.''

He heard her sigh faintly, but he didn't turn when she spoke.

"Ben...it's all wrong. I'm not right for you. I'm...not anything you need.''

"You're everything I need,'' he said with painful honesty.

"But you want to fill a house with kids, and I could lie and say I want that, too, but...I don't. And I couldn't do that to you.''

He turned then, needing to look at her face, and he saw tears on her cheeks. Staying where he was, he said softly, "I want a family, Reggie. A family. And I finally figured out it isn't in numbers. It's loving. Period.'' He spread his hands. "You and Mikey... I love you both. If that's all I have in life, it's more than enough. It's more than I've ever had before.''

Reggie stared at Ben, his words dropping into her being one by one and filling in corners of her soul that she had never known were empty. "You...you really mean that?''

"More than anything I've ever said in my life,'' he told her in a rough whisper. "But I'm not stupid. I know that Dennis is in the picture.''

"Oh, Ben,'' she murmured, unable to stop the tears that slipped down her cheeks. "I've been so wrong.'' The magnitude of her mistakes overwhelmed her. "I thought that all you wanted...that you had to have...''

He came closer to her, then touched her cheek with the tips of his fingers. "Just answer me one question.''

She nodded, a jerky movement, but couldn't say a word.

"Could you love me, Reggie?" Before she could answer him, he held up a hand to stop her. "No, let me rephrase that. Could you love me and Mikey? You know, love me, love my son?"

The world seemed to be holding its breath while Reggie just drank in the sight of Ben in front of her. She couldn't say the words, not when the lump in her throat was so huge. All she could do was go to Ben and hold on to him as if her life depended on it, because it did.

"Reggie?" he asked, and she could feel his arms trembling around her.

As her world settled into a place that it seemed she'd been looking for forever, Reggie tipped her head back and through tears smiled. "Oh, Ben, 'love' just doesn't seem like a big enough word for what I feel for you . . . and for Mikey."

"Are you sure? Dennis . . . and everything?"

"Dennis is gone. How could I have even considered marrying him, when I love you?" she breathed.

Any more words were lost in his kiss, a deep, searing connection that rocked her world. She held to him, returning kiss for kiss, feeling a freedom to taste and explore him that was stunning. When he drew back, she could tell that he wanted her as much as she wanted him. And his voice was rough with that need.

"If this weren't the hospital and if someone wouldn't be barging in here any moment, I'd . . ." He kissed her again, then pulled away. "And there are no locks on the door."

She managed a shaky laugh at that. "Too bad."

"Oh, yes, too bad," he whispered, then reached toward her, but not to hold her. Instead he began undoing the buttons on her silk blouse one by one, until the ruined fabric parted and slid off her shoulders to the floor.

"I think we both need a shower." He moved away. "You go first."

She fumbled with the snap on her slacks, slid them down, then stepped out of them. "We'll have time later," she said.

They stood facing each other in the soft light, then Ben drew her into his arms. "Oh, yes, we'll have the rest of our lives," he said.

And Reggie knew what her life was going to be about. Family. Her family. Ben and Mikey. She'd finally found what she'd been looking for... her home.

ANGELINA FADED back and out of sight; the sheer rush of success was a powerful feeling. Until she felt herself being zapped again. This time she came face-to-face with Miss Victoria, and the expression she met was anything but congratulatory.

"We are not amused by your tactics, Angelina. It is an unwritten law that no one, especially a small child, shall be injured in any way to further the progress of a mission."

Angelina didn't know what to say. If she admitted that the happenings of the past four hours weren't any of her doing, that Ben and Reggie had found themselves on their own, Miss Victoria would feel she hadn't done her job. Her plans weren't even in place yet, and wouldn't be until tonight. But now they wouldn't be needed.

But if she took credit for their coming together, everyone would think she'd sacrificed that dear child for the sake of love. A quandary, for sure. Then Miss Victoria settled it for Angelina.

"We will not pursue this, since the child is going to be just fine, but on future assignments, you will control your urges to break the rules. Or..."

Her voice trailed off, with the threat unsaid, but very potent. Angelina did not want to be in records. Not again.

"Yes, ma'am," she murmured, then ventured kudos to Miss Victoria to help smooth the rough spots a bit. "You were right about Regina and Benjamin, ma'am."

An imperious eyebrow was raised in her direction. "But of course."

Angelina nodded. "Now, if you don't need me for anything else...?"

Miss Victoria waved her hand at Angelina. "Very well, go. Do the finishing touches, and be sure to do your usual six-month check-up on the situation."

"Yes, ma'am."

She turned to go to the door to leave in the normal manner, but barely got to the entrance before she heard, "Oh, Angelina?"

"Report back here in...oh...a day of human time for your next assignment."

Angelina turned to look back at Miss Victoria. "Next assignment?" she asked.

"Yes, we have decided that more good came out of this than we first thought." She smiled at Angelina. "We believe that Mr. Benning and Melanie Clark might just be a match made in—"

Angelina stared in horror at Miss Victoria as she spoke calmly, then blurted out, "Oh, no."

Miss Victoria narrowed her eyes, then came toward Angelina. "Oh, yes."

Epilogue

Six months later

Reggie heard the phone ring twice while she was in the shower, then a muffled "I'll get it" from Ben in the Eaton master bedroom. No, the Grant master bedroom. She waited, hoping against hope that it wasn't the hospital calling again. Mikey was asleep and the house was theirs. And she wanted Ben. She never got enough of him. And she needed to tell him something, too. Something that he'd never believe.

She reached to turn off the water, but stopped when the shower-stall door clicked open, then Ben was there. Naked, smiling, that expression in his eyes that took her breath away.

"How about some company?" he asked as he stepped into the stall.

She smiled at him, something that she did a lot when she looked at him. "Sure, there's plenty of room," she murmured as he came close.

"You know," he said as he reached for the soap and rubbed it between his hands. "I think the guy who invented shower stalls should have a national day named after him.''

"Just like the guy who invented fireplaces?'' she asked with a smile. But her expression faltered when Ben reached out and started spreading the slippery soap on her body with his hands. On her shoulders, down to her arms, then on her breasts. "Yes...a ...a good idea,'' she managed as her breathing started to grow ragged.

He spanned her waist with his hands, then drew her toward him. "I bet he never guessed what some people would love to do in here.''

She put her arms around Ben and rested her face against his naked chest, letting the water stream around them. "Oh, maybe that's why he invented them.''

"That raunchy little rascal,'' he said with a rough laugh.

She tipped her head back to look at him, at his lashes spiked with water, his eyes so blue, his hair dark and flattened to his head. God, she loved him. "No, a bright man,'' she murmured.

When Ben kissed her, it never ceased to amaze her that her desire for her husband just never died. It grew with each encounter, and rose to new heights that she'd never explored before. He cupped his hands around her bottom and lifted her up against him, and she knew his desire for her was as real and urgent as hers for him.

She went to him, knowing so much about him, but finding something new every time. She loved him, but love just never seemed to cover all her feelings. She needed him, wanted him, missed him when he was gone, loved everything about him. And despite her fears, she loved Mikey, too.

"You know, that woman you lived with was right. Love just expands to include more. It doesn't diminish," she whispered in his ear. He lifted her higher, then slowly, ever so slowly, he slid into her. Braced against the side of the shower, he helped her raise and lower on him, the feelings raw and urgent, growing until she threw her head back and let go.

Gradually she came back to reality, to being held by Ben, water running over them. Then she kissed him, deep and long.

"Boy," he whispered, "Just once I'd like to get in here to take a shower."

She laughed at that, an easy, free expression, then Ben was carrying her out of the stall, letting her grab two towels on the way into the shadowy bedroom. He laid her down on the big poster bed, then he caught the towel she tossed him. As he roughly dried himself, Reggie toweled her hair and then sat up cross-legged on the bed.

Ben threw his towel to the foot of the bed, then climbed up on the bed to face Reggie on his knees in the rumpled sheets. "So, tell me again about love."

She touched his thigh, then drew back. "Something's happened." She bit her lip, then blurted out, "I'm pregnant."

Ben stared at her and uttered one word. "How?"

She could almost smile at that. "You're the doctor. You must know about—"

He moved abruptly, coming closer, close enough to cup her chin in his hand, and she could feel how unsteady his touch was.

"I know all that, but what I meant was we took precautions. I don't understand . . ." He slowly pulled back from her. "I'm sorry, Reggie," he said in a low voice.

"Sorry?" She moved to him, touching his chest with her hands, smoothing the damp hair and wondering how life could be so strange, yet so wonderful at the same time. "Ben, I never—"

He cut her off when he covered her hands with his. "I know—you never wanted more kids. I mean, Mikey keeps you busy all the time, and even with Nancy helping, it's hard sometimes."

He moved back from her, then got off the bed and looked confused for a minute, then turned back to her. The shadows touched his face, but she could see something there that made her ache.

"I'm just sorry, that's all."

She scrambled off the bed and went to him, making contact again by taking his hand in hers. "It's all true what you said, but something really remarkable has happened. I don't understand it myself. When I went to the doctor, I thought I was run-down. Tired, sleepy, that sort of thing. Then he told me I wasn't sick. I was just very pregnant—nine weeks along to be exact.

"I was so shocked. I never thought of that. Then he told me that no birth control is a hundred percent sure. A little bit like locking the barn door after the horse gets out." She actually laughed softly at that. "He didn't think it was funny. Actually, I didn't, either, at the time." She couldn't tell Ben that she'd cried at first, before she'd realized that it wasn't the catastrophe she'd thought it would be. "But now I do."

Ben took his hand out of hers, then touched her on her shoulders, not exactly holding her, but just touching, being there. "Reggie, what are we going to do?"

She could almost see him holding his breath, and she couldn't bear the way his mouth was set or his eyes had narrowed. She reached up and smoothed the lines at his mouth with the tips of her fingers. "I think we're going to be parents again," she whispered, as her fingers stilled on his jaw. "But this time you won't have forms to fill out."

"Are you serious?" he asked in a raspy whisper.

She got even closer and kissed his chest right above his heart. "Very serious," she breathed against his warm skin.

His fingers tangled in her hair, and he eased her head back so she was looking up into remarkable blue eyes.

"You don't have to do this, you know."

"I know I don't. But I want to. I won't pretend that I was trying for this, but now that it's happened, I realized that I think Mikey should have a brother or a sister. And do you know what?"

"What?" he asked.

"I want to have your child." She tried to smile, but her emotions were so overwhelming that she could barely think straight. "It's a miracle, and I'm not questioning it. I never thought I'd feel this way, but then again, I've never loved anyone the way I love you. It just seems so right. Magic, Ben, pure and simple.''

He kissed her, a quick, searing contact, then drew back and echoed, ''Magic, pure and simple.''

Then she was in his arms, being held and loved, and she knew that she was right where she was supposed to be, but just hadn't known it before.

Ben carried her back to the bed, then they collapsed back onto the sheets together. Then he was looking down at her, propping his head on one hand. ''I'm stunned,'' he told her.

''But happy?'' she asked.

''That's a given, Reggie,'' he said as his hand skimmed over the line of her hip to rest on her thigh. ''Oh, I almost forgot. The phone call.''

She covered his hand on her with her hand and said, ''No, no hospital, not right now.''

''No, it's not that. The phone call was from—'' His words were cut off by a knocking on the door.

''Dr. Grant,'' Nancy said through the wooden barrier.

''Yes, Nancy.''

''It's Mikey. He's upset and he wants—''

''I'll be right there.''

''No, sir. He wants Mrs. Grant. He keeps saying he wants his mommy.''

Reggie grinned at Ben. ''Sorry, my son's calling for me,'' she said, then scooted off the bed and reached for her robe.

As she hurried to the door, Ben called after her, ''I'm waiting.''

She blew him a kiss over her shoulder, then knotted the tie on her robe and reached for the door.

"Darling, the phone call. Don't you want to know who it was?"

She opened the door, then glanced back at Ben, who was sitting on the edge of the bed, watching her with a strange expression on his face. "Okay, I give up, who was it?"

"Melanie. She wants you to call her first thing in the morning."

She frowned. "Why? Is something wrong?"

He shrugged. "I don't know. She said to tell you she's going out with Mr. Perfect and she'll give you a full rundown on the evening in the morning."

Reggie could feel her mouth drop. Dennis and Mel?

Right then Mikey yelled, "Mommy. Want my mommy!"

She glanced down the hallway, then back at Ben. "I'll be right back." She hurried toward Mikey's room. "Mel and Dennis," she muttered. "When cows fly."

ANGELINA WATCHED Reggie go into the boy's room, then withdrew with a smile. Reggie had no way of knowing that cows had already flown once, and they just might again.

1997

Reader's Engagement Book
A calendar of important dates
and anniversaries for readers to use!

Informative and entertaining—with notable
dates and trivia highlighted throughout the year.

Handy, convenient, pocketbook size to help you
keep track of your own personal important dates.

Added bonus—contains $5.00 worth of coupons
for upcoming Harlequin and Silhouette books.
This calendar more than pays for itself!

Available beginning in November at
your favorite retail outlet.

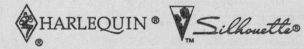

HARLEQUIN ®   Silhouette®

Merry Christmas, Baby!

A romantic collection filled with the magic
of Christmas and the joy of children.

SUSAN WIGGS, Karen Young and
Bobby Hutchinson bring you Christmas wishes,
weddings and romance, in a charming
trio of stories that will warm up your
holiday season.

MERRY CHRISTMAS, BABY! also contains
Harlequin's special gift to you—a set of
FREE GIFT TAGS included in every book.

Brighten up your holiday season with
MERRY CHRISTMAS, BABY!

Available in November at
your favorite retail store.

HARLEQUIN ®

Look us up on-line at: http://www.romance.net   MCB

Maybe This Time...

Maybe this time...they'll get what they really wanted all those years ago. Whether it's the man who got away, a baby, or a new lease on life, these four women will get a second chance at a once-in-a-lifetime opportunity!

Four top-selling authors have come together to make you believe that in the world of American Romance anything is possible:

#642 ONE HUSBAND TOO MANY
Jacqueline Diamond
August

#646 WHEN A MAN LOVES A WOMAN
Bonnie K. Winn
September

#650 HEAVEN CAN WAIT
Emily Dalton
October

#654 THE COMEBACK MOM
Muriel Jensen
November

Look us up on-line at: http://www.romance.net

MTTG

REBECCA
43 LIGHT STREET
YORK
FACE TO FACE

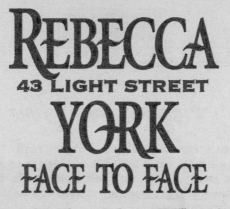

Bestselling author Rebecca York returns to "43 Light Street"
for an original story of past secrets, deadly deceptions—and
the most intimate betrayal.

She woke in a hospital—with amnesia...and with child.
According to her rescuer, whose striking face is the last
image she remembers, she's Justine Hollingsworth. But
nothing about her life seems to fit, except for the baby
inside her and Mike Lancer's arms around her. Consumed
by forbidden passion and racked by nameless fear, she
must discover if she is Justine...or the victim of some mind
game. Her life—and her unborn child's—depends on it....

Don't miss *Face To Face*—Available in October, wherever
Harlequin books are sold.

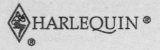

HARLEQUIN ®

43FTF